MONSTROUS TALES

Monstrous Tales

Stories of Strange Creatures and Fearsome Beasts from around the World

ILLUSTRATIONS BY
Sija Hong

CHRONICLE BOOKS
SAN FRANCISCO

Library of Congress Cataloging-in-Publication Data
Names: Hong, Sija, illustrator.
Title: Monstrous tales : stories of strange creatures and fearsome beasts
    from around the world / illustrated by Sija Hong.
Description: San Francisco : Chronicle Books, [2020] | Includes
    bibliographical references. | Summary: "This collection of traditional
    folktales crawls with bewitching and blood-thirsty creatures, and each
    story is paired with spellbinding contemporary art in this special
    illustrated edition"-- Provided by publisher.
Identifiers: LCCN 2019047179 | ISBN 9781452182599 (hardback)
Subjects: LCSH: Fairy tales. | Monsters--Folklore. | Tales. | CYAC: Fairy
    tales. | Monsters--Folklore. | Folklore.
Classification: LCC PZ8 .M756 2020 | DDC 398.2--dc23
    LC record available at https://lccn.loc.gov/2019047179

ISBN 978-1-4521-8259-9

Manufactured in China.

Design by AJ Hansen.

Illustrations by Sija Hong.

10 9 8 7 6 5 4

Chronicle books and gifts are available at special quantity discounts to corporations,
professional associations, literacy programs, and other organizations. For details and discount
information, please contact our premiums department at corporatesales@chroniclebooks.com
or at 1-800-759-0190.

Chronicle Books LLC
680 Second Street
San Francisco, California 94107
www.chroniclebooks.com

"At last he began to take courage, and moved on softly step by step.
What he saw was creepier than creepy, and surpassed all he had ever dreamt of."

—FRIEDRICH KREUTZWALD, TRANSLATED BY LEONORA LANG,
"The Young Man Who Would Have His Eyes Opened"

CONTENTS

After Dark

MY LORD BAG of RICE

❖

Japan

Long, long ago there lived in Japan a brave warrior known to all as Tawara Toda, or "My Lord Bag of Rice." His true name was Fujiwara Hidesato, and there is a very interesting story of how he came to change his name.

One day he sallied forth in search of adventures, for he had the nature of a warrior and could not bear to be idle. So he buckled on his two swords, took his huge bow, much taller than himself, in his hand, and slinging his quiver on his back started out. He had not gone far when he came to the bridge of Seta-no-Karashi spanning one end of the beautiful Lake Biwa. No sooner had he set foot on the bridge than he saw lying right across his path a huge serpent-dragon. Its body was so big that it looked like the trunk of a large pine tree and it took up the whole width of the bridge. One of its huge claws rested on the parapet of one side of the bridge, while its tail lay right against the other. The monster seemed to be asleep, and as it breathed, fire and smoke came out of its nostrils.

At first Hidesato could not help feeling alarmed at the sight of this horrible reptile lying in his path, for he must either turn back or walk right over its body. He was a brave man, however, and putting aside all fear went forward dauntlessly. Crunch, crunch! he stepped now on the dragon's body, now between its coils, and without even one glance backward he went on his way.

He had only gone a few steps when he heard some one calling him from behind. On turning back he was much surprised to see that the monster dragon had entirely disappeared and in its place was a strange-looking man, who was bowing most ceremoniously to the ground. His red hair streamed over his shoulders and was surmounted by a crown in the shape of a dragon's head, and his sea-green dress was patterned with shells. Hidesato knew at once that this was no ordinary mortal and he wondered much at the strange occurrence. Where had the dragon gone in such a short space of time? Or had it transformed itself into this man, and what did the whole thing mean? While these thoughts passed through his mind he had come up to the man on the bridge and now addressed him:

"Was it you that called me just now?"

"Yes, it was I," answered the man: "I have an earnest request to make to you. Do you think you can grant it to me?"

"If it is in my power to do so I will," answered Hidesato, "but first tell me who you are?"

"I am the Dragon King of the Lake, and my home is in these waters just under this bridge."

"And what is it you have to ask of me?" said Hidesato.

"I want you to kill my mortal enemy the centipede, who lives on the mountain beyond," and the Dragon King pointed to a high peak on the opposite shore of the lake.

"I have lived now for many years in this lake and I have a large family of children and grandchildren. For some time past we have lived in terror, for a monster centipede has discovered our home, and night after night it comes and carries off one of my family. I am powerless to save them. If it goes on much longer like this, not only shall I lose all my children, but I myself must fall a victim to the monster. I am, therefore, very unhappy, and in my extremity I determined to ask the help of a human being. For many days with this intention I have waited on the bridge in the shape of the horrible serpent-dragon that you saw, in the hope that some strong brave man would come along. But all who came this way, as soon as they saw me were terrified and ran away as fast as they could. You are the first man I have found able to look at me without fear, so I knew at once that you were a man of great courage. I beg you to have pity upon me. Will you not help me and kill my enemy the centipede?"

Hidesato felt very sorry for the Dragon King on hearing his story, and readily promised to do what he could to help him. The warrior asked where the centipede lived, so that he might attack the creature at once. The Dragon King replied that its home was on the mountain Mikami, but that as it came every night at a certain hour to the palace of the lake, it would be better to wait till then. So Hidesato was conducted to the palace of the Dragon King, under the bridge. Strange to say, as he followed his host downwards the waters parted to let them pass, and his clothes did not even feel damp as he passed through the flood. Never had Hidesato seen anything so beautiful as this palace built of white marble beneath the lake. He had often heard of the Sea King's palace at the bottom of the sea, where all the servants and retainers were salt-water fishes, but here was a magnificent building in the heart of Lake Biwa. The dainty goldfishes, red carp, and silvery trout waited upon the Dragon King and his guest.

Hidesato was astonished at the feast that was spread for him. The dishes were crystallized lotus leaves and flowers, and the chopsticks were of the rarest ebony. As soon as they sat down, the sliding doors opened and ten lovely goldfish dancers came out, and behind them followed ten red-carp musicians with the koto and the samisen. Thus the hours flew by till midnight, and the beautiful music and dancing had banished all thoughts of the centipede. The Dragon King was about to pledge the warrior in a fresh cup of wine when the palace was suddenly shaken by a tramp, tramp! as if a mighty army had begun to march not far away.

Hidesato and his host both rose to their feet and rushed to the balcony, and the warrior saw on the opposite mountain two great balls of glowing fire coming nearer and nearer. The Dragon King stood by the warrior's side trembling with fear.

"The centipede! The centipede! Those two balls of fire are its eyes. It is coming for its prey! Now is the time to kill it."

Hidesato looked where his host pointed, and, in the dim light of the starlit evening, behind the two balls of fire he saw the long body of an enormous centipede winding round the mountains, and the light in its hundred feet glowed like so many distant lanterns moving slowly towards the shore.

Hidesato showed not the least sign of fear. He tried to calm the Dragon King.

"Don't be afraid. I shall surely kill the centipede. Just bring me my bow and arrows."

The Dragon King did as he was bid, and the warrior noticed that he had only three arrows left in his quiver. He took the bow, and fitting an arrow to the notch, took careful aim and let fly.

The arrow hit the centipede right in the middle of its head, but instead of penetrating, it glanced off harmless and fell to the ground.

Nothing daunted, Hidesato took another arrow, fitted it to the notch of the bow and let fly. Again the arrow hit the mark, it struck the centipede right in the middle of its head, only to glance off and fall to the ground. The centipede was invulnerable to weapons! When the Dragon King saw that even this brave warrior's arrows were powerless to kill the centipede, he lost heart and began to tremble with fear.

The warrior saw that he had now only one arrow left in his quiver, and if this one failed he could not kill the centipede. He looked across the waters. The huge reptile had wound its horrid body seven times round the mountain and would soon come down to the lake. Nearer and nearer gleamed fireballs of eyes, and the light of its hundred feet began to throw reflections in the still waters of the lake.

Then suddenly the warrior remembered that he had heard that human saliva was deadly to centipedes. But this was no ordinary centipede. This was so monstrous that even to think of such a creature made one creep with horror. Hidesato determined to try his last chance. So taking his last arrow and first putting the end of it in his mouth, he fitted the notch to his bow, took careful aim once more and let fly.

This time the arrow again hit the centipede right in the middle of its head, but instead of glancing off harmlessly as before, it struck home to the creature's brain. Then with a convulsive shudder the serpentine body stopped moving, and the fiery light of its great eyes and hundred feet darkened to a dull glare like the sunset of a stormy day, and then went out in blackness. A great darkness now overspread the heavens, the thunder rolled and the lightning flashed, and the wind roared in fury, and it seemed as if the world were coming to an end. The Dragon King and his children and retainers all crouched in different parts of the palace, frightened to death, for the building was shaken to its foundation. At last the dreadful night was over. Day dawned beautiful and clear. The centipede was gone from the mountain.

Then Hidesato called to the Dragon King to come out with him on the balcony, for the centipede was dead and he had nothing more to fear.

Then all the inhabitants of the palace came out with joy, and Hidesato pointed to the lake. There lay the body of the dead centipede floating on the water, which was dyed red with its blood.

The gratitude of the Dragon King knew no bounds. The whole family came and bowed down before the warrior, calling him their preserver and the bravest warrior in all Japan.

Another feast was prepared, more sumptuous than the first. All kinds of fish, prepared in every imaginable way, raw, stewed, boiled and roasted, served on coral trays and crystal dishes, were put before him, and the wine was the best that Hidesato had ever tasted in his life. To add to the beauty of everything the sun shone brightly, the lake glittered like a liquid diamond, and the palace was a thousand times more beautiful by day than by night.

His host tried to persuade the warrior to stay a few days, but Hidesato insisted on going home, saying that he had now finished what he had come to do, and must return. The Dragon King and his family were all very sorry to have him leave so soon, but since he would go they begged him to accept a few small presents (so they said) in token of their gratitude to him for delivering them forever from their horrible enemy the centipede.

As the warrior stood in the porch taking leave, a train of fish was suddenly transformed into a retinue of men, all wearing ceremonial robes and dragon's crowns on their heads to show that they were servants of the great Dragon King. The presents that they carried were as follows:

First, a large bronze bell.
Second, a bag of rice.
Third, a roll of silk.
Fourth, a cooking pot.
Fifth, a bell.

Hidesato did not want to accept all these presents, but as the Dragon King insisted, he could not well refuse.

The Dragon King himself accompanied the warrior as far as the bridge, and then took leave of him with many bows and good wishes, leaving the procession of servants to accompany Hidesato to his house with the presents.

The warrior's household and servants had been very much concerned when they found that he did not return the night before, but they finally concluded that he had been kept by the violent storm and had taken shelter somewhere. When the servants on the watch for his return caught sight of him they called to every one that he was approaching, and the whole household turned out to meet him, wondering much what the retinue of men, bearing presents and banners, that followed him, could mean.

As soon as the Dragon King's retainers had put down the presents they vanished, and Hidesato told all that had happened to him.

The presents which he had received from the grateful Dragon King were found to be of magic power. The bell only was ordinary, and as Hidesato had no use for it he presented it to the temple near by, where it was hung up, to boom out the hour of day over the surrounding neighborhood.

The single bag of rice, however much was taken from it day after day for the meals of the knight and his whole family, never grew less—the supply in the bag was inexhaustible.

The roll of silk, too, never grew shorter, though time after time long pieces were cut off to make the warrior a new suit of clothes to go to Court in at the New Year.

The cooking pot was wonderful, too. No matter what was put into it, it cooked deliciously whatever was wanted without any firing—truly a very economical saucepan.

The fame of Hidesato's fortune spread far and wide, and as there was no need for him to spend money on rice or silk or firing, he became very rich and prosperous, and was henceforth known as *My Lord Bag of Rice*.

THE BLOOD-DRAWING GHOST

Ireland

There was a young man in the parish of Drimalegue, county Cork, who was courting three girls at one time, and he didn't know which of them would he take; they had equal fortunes, and any of the three was as pleasing to him as any other. One day when he was coming home from the fair with his two sisters, the sisters began:

"Well, John," said one of them, "why don't you get married. Why don't you take either Mary, or Peggy, or Kate?"

"I can't tell you that," said John, "till I find which of them has the best wish for me."

"How will you know?" asked the other.

"I will tell you that as soon as any person will die in the parish." In three weeks' time from that day an old man died. John went to the wake and then to the funeral. While they were burying the corpse in the graveyard John stood near a tomb which was next to the grave, and when all were going away, after burying the old man, he remained standing a while by himself, as if thinking of something; then he put his blackthorn stick on top of the tomb, stood a while longer, and on going from the graveyard left the stick behind him. He went home and ate his supper. After supper John went to a neighbour's house where young people used to meet of an evening, and the three girls happened to be there that time. John was very quiet, so that every one noticed him.

"What is troubling you this evening, John?" asked one of the girls.

"Oh, I am sorry for my beautiful blackthorn," said he.

"Did you lose it?"

"I did not," said John; "but I left it on the top of the tomb next to the grave of the man who was buried to-day, and whichever of you three will go for it is the woman I'll marry. Well, Mary will you go for my stick?" asked he.

"Faith, then, I will not," said Mary.

"Well, Peggy, will you go?"

"If I were without a man for ever," said Peggy, "I wouldn't go."

"Well, Kate," said he to the third, "will you go for my stick? If you go I'll marry you."

"Stand to your word," said Kate, "and I'll bring the stick."

"Believe me, that I will," said John.

Kate left the company behind her, and went for the stick. The graveyard was three miles away and the walk was a long one. Kate came to the place at last and made out the tomb by the fresh grave. When she had her hand on the blackthorn a voice called from the tomb:

"Leave the stick where it is and open this tomb for me."

Kate began to tremble and was greatly in dread, but something was forcing her to open the tomb—she couldn't help herself.

"Take the lid off now," said the dead man when Kate had the door open and was inside in the tomb, "and take me out of this—take me on your back."

Afraid to refuse, she took the lid from the coffin, raised the dead man on her back, and walked on in the way he directed. She walked about the distance of a mile. The load, being very heavy, was near breaking her back and killing her. She walked half a mile farther and came to a village; the houses were at the side of the road.

"Take me to the first house," said the dead man.

She took him.

"Oh, we cannot go in here," said he, when they came near. "The people have clean water inside, and they have holy water, too. Take me to the next house."

She went to the next house.

"We cannot go in there," said he, when she stopped in front of the door. "They have clean water, and there is holy water as well."

She went to the third house.

"Go in here," said the dead man. "There is neither clean water nor holy water in this place; we can stop in it."

They went in.

"Bring a chair now and put me sitting at the side of the fire. Then find me something to eat and to drink."

She placed him in a chair by the hearth, searched the house, found a dish of oatmeal and brought it. "I have nothing to give you to drink but dirty water," said she.

"Bring me a dish and a razor."

She brought the dish and the razor.

"Come, now," said he, "to the room above."

They went up to the room, where three young men, sons of the man of the house, were sleeping in bed, and Kate had to hold the dish while the dead man was drawing their blood.

"Let the father and mother have that," said he, "in return for the dirty water"; meaning that if there was clean water in the house he wouldn't have taken the blood of the young men. He closed their wounds in the way that there was no sign of a cut on them. "Mix this now with the meal, get a dish of it for yourself and another for me."

She got two plates and put the oatmeal in it after mixing it, and brought two spoons. Kate wore a handkerchief on her head; she put this under her neck and tied it; she was pretending to eat, but she was putting the food to hide in the handkerchief till her plate was empty.

"Have you your share eaten?" asked the dead man.

"I have," answered Kate.

"I'll have mine finished this minute," said he, and soon after he gave her the empty dish. She put the dishes back in the dresser, and didn't mind washing them. "Come, now," said he, "and take me back to the place where you found me."

"Oh, how can I take you back; you are too great a load; 'twas killing me you were when I brought you." She was in dread of going from the house again.

"You are stronger after that food than what you were in coming; take me back to my grave."

She went against her will. She rolled up the food inside the handkerchief. There was a deep hole in the wall of the kitchen by the door, where the bar was slipped in when they barred the door; into this hole she put the handkerchief. In going back she shortened the road by going through a big field at command of the dead man. When they were at the top of the field she asked, was there any cure for those young men whose blood was drawn?

"There is no cure," said he, "except one. If any of that food had been spared, three bits of it in each young man's mouth would bring them to life again, and they'd never know of their death."

"Then," said Kate in her own mind, "that cure is to be had."

"Do you see this field?" asked the dead man.

"I do."

"Well, there is as much gold buried in it as would make rich people of all who belong to you. Do you see the three leachtans [piles of small stones]? Underneath each of them is a pot of gold."

The dead man looked around for a while; then Kate went on, without stopping, till she came to the wall of the graveyard, and just then they heard the cock crow.

"The cock is crowing," said Kate; "it's time for me to be going home."

"It is not time yet," said the dead man; "that is a bastard cock."

A moment after that another cock crowed. "There the cocks are crowing a second time," said she. "No," said the dead man, "that is a bastard cock again; that's no right bird." They came to the mouth of the tomb and a cock crowed the third time.

"Well," said the girl, "that must be the right cock."

"Ah, my girl, that cock has saved your life for you. But for him I would have you with me in the grave for evermore, and if I knew this cock would crow before I was in the grave you wouldn't have the knowledge you have now of the field and the gold. Put me into the coffin where you found me. Take your time and settle me well. I cannot meddle with you now, and 'tis sorry I am to part with you."

"Will you tell me who you are?" asked Kate.

"Have you ever heard your father or mother mention a man called Edward Derrihy or his son Michael?"

"It's often I heard tell of them," replied the girl.

"Well, Edward Derrihy was my father; I am Michael. That blackthorn that you came for to-night to this graveyard was the lucky stick for you, but if you had any thought of the danger that was before you, you wouldn't be here. Settle me carefully and close the tomb well behind you."

She placed him in the coffin carefully, closed the door behind her, took the blackthorn stick, and away home with Kate. The night was far spent when she came. She was tired, and it's good reason the girl had. She thrust the stick into the thatch above the door of the house and rapped. Her sister rose up and opened the door.

"Where did you spend the night?" asked the sister. "Mother will kill you in the morning for spending the whole night from home."

"Go to bed," answered Kate, "and never mind me."

They went to bed, and Kate fell asleep the minute she touched the bed, she was that tired after the night.

When the father and mother of the three young men rose next morning, and there was no sign of their sons, the mother went to the room to call them, and there she found the three dead. She began to screech and wring her hands. She ran to the road screaming and wailing. All the neighbours crowded around to know what trouble was on her. She told them her three sons were lying dead in their bed after the night. Very soon the report spread in every direction. When Kate's father and mother heard it they hurried off to the house of the dead men. When they came home Kate was still in bed; the mother took a stick and began to beat the girl for being out all the night and in bed all the day.

"Get up now, you lazy stump of a girl," said she, "and go to the wake house; your neighbour's three sons are dead."

Kate took no notice of this. "I am very tired and sick," said she. "You'd better spare me and give me a drink."

The mother gave her a drink of milk and a bite to eat, and in the middle of the day she rose up.

"'Tis a shame for you not to be at the wake house yet," said the mother; "hurry over now."

When Kate reached the house there was a great crowd of people before her and great wailing. She did not cry, but was looking on. The father was as if wild, going up and down the house wringing his hands.

"Be quiet," said Kate. "Control yourself."

"How can I do that, my dear girl, and my three fine sons lying dead in the house?"

"What would you give," asked Kate, "to the person who would bring life to them again?"

"Don't be vexing me," said the father.

"It's neither vexing you I am nor trifling," said Kate. "I can put the life in them again."

"If it was true that you could do that, I would give you all that I have inside the house and outside as well."

"All I want from you," said Kate, "is the eldest son to marry and Gort na Leachtan [the field of the stone heaps] as fortune."

"My dear, you will have that from me with the greatest blessing."

"Give me the field in writing from yourself, whether the son will marry me or not."

He gave her the field in his handwriting. She told all who were inside in the wake-house to go outside the door, every man and woman of them. Some were laughing at her and more were crying, thinking it was mad she was. She bolted the door inside, and went to the place where she left the handkerchief, found it, and put three bites of the oatmeal and the blood in the mouth of each young man, and as soon as she did that the three got their natural colour, and they looked like men sleeping. She opened the door, then called on all to come inside, and told the father to go and wake his sons.

He called each one by name, and as they woke they seemed very tired after their night's rest; they put on their clothes, and were greatly surprised to see all the people around. "How is this?" asked the eldest brother.

"Don't you know of anything that came over you in the night?" asked the father.

"We do not," said the sons. "We remember nothing at all since we fell asleep last evening."

The father then told them everything, but they could not believe it. Kate went away home and told her father and mother of her night's journey to and from the graveyard, and said that she would soon tell them more.

That day she met John.

"Did you bring the stick?" asked he.

"Find your own stick," said she, "and never speak to me again in your life."

In a week's time she went to the house of the three young men, and said to the father, "I have come for what you promised me."

"You'll get that with my blessing," said the father. He called the eldest son aside then and asked would he marry Kate, their neighbour's daughter. "I will," said the son. Three days after that the two were married and had a fine wedding. For three weeks they enjoyed a pleasant life without toil or trouble; then Kate said, "This will not do for us; we must be working. Come with me to-morrow and I'll give yourself and brothers plenty to do, and my own father and brothers as well."

She took them next day to one of the stone heaps in Gort na Leachtan. "Throw these stones to one side," said she.

They thought that she was losing her senses, but she told them that they'd soon see for themselves what she was doing. They went to work and kept at it till they had six feet deep of a hole dug; then they met with a flat stone three feet square and an iron hook in the middle of it.

"Sure there must be something underneath this," said the men. They lifted the flag, and under it was a pot of gold. All were very happy then. "There is more gold yet in the place," said Kate. "Come, now, to the other heap." They removed that heap, dug down, and found another pot of gold. They removed the third pile and found a third pot full of gold. On the side of the third pot was an inscription, and they could not make out what it was. After emptying it they placed the pot by the side of the door.

About a month later a poor scholar walked the way, and as he was going in at the door he saw the old pot and the letters on the side of it. He began to study the letters.

"You must be a good scholar if you can read what's on that pot," said the young man.

"I can," said the poor scholar, "and here it is for you. There is a deal more at the south side of each pot."

The young man said nothing, but putting his hand in his pocket, gave the poor scholar a good day's hire. When he was gone they went to work and found a deal more of gold in the south side of each stone heap. They were very happy then and very rich, and bought several farms and built fine houses, and it was supposed by all of them in the latter end that it was Derrihy's money that was buried under the leachtans, but they could give no correct account of that, and sure why need they care? When they died they left property to make their children rich to the seventh generation.

THE DEMON'S DAUGHTER

Syria

nce upon a time, there were three sisters who had neither father nor mother. They washed wool, and every day the eldest went to the market and sold it, and with the money, she bought what they needed to drink and eat.

One evening, when the sisters were at home, they heard the muezzin calling the sundown prayer, and the youngest said to the eldest, "Get up and light the lamp." She began searching for matches, but finding none, she took the lamp and climbed up to the terrace to go get a light from the neighbors. She went from house to house until she came to a terrace she didn't know.

She looked around her and found forty-one lamps lit, forty small ones and one big one. She lit her lamp from this one, but immediately she heard a voice coming from the lamp and saying, "You took fire from me; you will bear my child."

The girl was still a virgin and she didn't worry over these words. When she returned to her sisters, they said, "Where have you been? We've been sitting here without a light while you were visiting with the neighbors."

"No, by God, I was not with the neighbors; but while I was looking for somewhere to light our lamp, something extraordinary happened to me. As I was walking along the terraces, I suddenly found myself in a place I didn't know, and there I saw forty small lamps and, in the their midst, one which was as big as the copper trough; I lit my lamp from it, but then it spoke to me: "You took fire from me; you will bear my child." The sisters replied: "Did you hear this with your own ears? Do lamps talk now?" And they refused to believe it.

But six months later they saw that their sister was big like a woman with child. The three sisters cried copiously over it. But one night, when nine months had passed and they were celebrating he whose eye never closes and who never sleeps, the wall cracked open and a demon emerged and greeted them—but they fainted in their fear. The demon, who understood that they were afraid of him, fetched water to sprinkle on their faces, until they came to. Then he said to them: "Don't be afraid, girls, I'm your eldest sister's husband. The moment has come for her to give birth, and I will assist her." With these words, he pulled a knife from his pocket and slit open his wife's side, saying: "Come, my daughter." And then the baby emerged from her mother's side.

Then he said to the mother: "Everything you desire—food, clothes, etc.—will be yours; you need only say to yourself: I want such and such thing, and immediately it will be ready, so that you need no longer wash wool or do any other work. I will go now, but in fifteen years I will see you again. Good bye, and may God protect you," he said, and with that the demon disappeared.

The woman raised her daughter, and every time she desired something, she received it, and thus fifteen years passed. One beautiful day, the daughter asked her mother to go out walking with her for a little while. They walked, and when they had sat down on the bank of the river, the girl rose to wash her hands, but with this movement she let fall a gold bracelet adorned with precious stones. The child burst into tears over her bracelet, but her mother said to her: "Don't fret; tomorrow we will go to the goldsmith, who will make you another; get up now, let's go back home."

They left, but later the king's son came to the same pathway and sat on the riverbank. He spotted something shining in the water and commanded one of his servants to go down and bring him back the bracelet. The servant obeyed, and after pulling it from the water, he gave it to the prince. The prince was very surprised by it and said to himself: "Ah, it is women like the mistress of this bracelet who are worth tears and complaints, and neither silver nor gold." Then he called his servants and ordered them to bring his horse. He mounted it without paying heed to anyone else and, sick and slumped over, he returned to the palace. When his mother asked him what was wrong, he replied: "Oh, mother, if you love me, you will bring me the mistress of this bracelet so that I may marry her."

She took the bracelet and began her search in all the streets of Damas; at every house she passed, she asked: "Is there anyone here to whom this bracelet belongs?" All admired the bracelet, but she always received a negative reply, until she arrived at a house in which she found a young girl who was as beautiful as the rising sun. When she had greeted the girl, and the girl had greeted her in return, she asked after the owner of the bracelet. "Yes, certainly I know her," the girl said, "it is I myself." Then her mother arrived, and as they conversed, the queen asked her if she would like to give her daughter's hand to the prince. She replied: "It is impossible for me to answer either yes or no; but when her father arrives, I'll consult with him, and tomorrow you will have our reply."

One hour had hardly passed since the queen left, when the wall cracked open and the demon emerged. When they had greeted each other and he had kissed his daughter, the mother told him of the queen's proposition and asked if he would consent. "Yes," he said, "but for the bride price, you must ask the fiancé for forty camel loads of silver; if he gives you this, you may marry off my daughter without hesitation."

Then he addressed his daughter: "I will give you a piece of advice which you must never neglect." And when she had assured him she would not, he continued: "When your husband visits you, you must not speak a word to him, until he says: 'I beseech you by your father, the master of the lamps.' If he says these words, you may speak to him, but if he does not, you will never speak to him, even if you stay with him for one hundred years." "By my head and by my eye," she said, and then the demon departed.

The next morning, the queen arrived and asked them for their definitive answer, and having heard it, she asked how much they wished for the bride price. After learning that they were asking for forty camel loads of silver, she returned and informed her son of this reply. Immediately he called his lackeys and ordered them to prepare the forty loads, and when everything was ready, he sent them with the soldiers and the lackeys and bade it be said that he wished to celebrate the marriage that very night.

When they had consented, he stayed in the palace until the evening, then presented himself at his fiancée's house. He found her as beautiful as the rising sun, but when he spoke to her, she did not reply. He was surprised and thought that she was mute, but when he recounted this to his mother the next day, she said: "No, my son, your wife is not mute, by God, she twitters like a bird."

They spent a year together in this way, but as she never spoke to him, he decided to marry a second woman. The new bride wished to see her rival; she went to visit her, and when she had greeted her, she returned the greeting and was not mute at all. "This is strange," the woman said to herself, "here is a girl such as this, who is married to the king's son, and who nevertheless never speaks to him." The demon's daughter called a slave and commanded her to bring the meal, so that she might dine with her guest—she did not know that it was the prince's concubine—and the slave brought them various dishes. But as she presented the dishes, she let one fall on the floor, and it broke. The dish was of emeralds and zircons and had no equal in the collections of all the kings of all the world. Seeing that it was broken, the mistress took a whip and began to whip the slave and continued until she cried out: "I am under the protection of your father, the master of the lamps." Hearing these words, her mistress stopped whipping and let her go.

The rival, who had heard them, went home and said to the king[1]: "Sire, today I visited your wife and I dined with her; she twitters like birds and is not mute at all. On the contrary, I observed a little episode: her slave, who was presenting the dishes to us, let one fall, and it broke; so her mistress took a whip and began to whip her, but the slave cried out: "I am under the protection of your father, the master of the lamps;" at those words, she suddenly stopped hitting her." The king meditated on these words and thought: "By God, I will say these words to her, and then perhaps she will talk." He went to her and said: "My dear, I am your slave, and I am going to die because of you; I beseech you by your father, the master of the lamps, speak to me, even if it is only one word." When she heard these words which her father had told her about, she replied to the king: "My dear, you are my soul and my heart," and the couple embraced each other.

Here is the end of the tale; if it is good, you will give me a round cake, and if it is not, you will hang me from the mulberry tree.

---

1. The same who is called the prince in the preceding text.

THE SOBBING PINE

Pueblo of Isleta

A mong the folk-lore heroes of whom every Quères lad has heard is Ees-tée-ah Muts, the Arrow Boy. He was a great hunter and did many remarkable things, but there was once a time when all his courage and strength were of no avail, when but for the help of a little squirrel he would have perished miserably.

On reaching manhood Ees-tée-ah Muts married the daughter of the Kot-chin (chief). She was a very beautiful girl and her hunter-husband was very fond of her. But, alas! she was secretly a witch and every night when Ees-tée-ah Muts was asleep she used to fly away to the mountains, where the witches held their uncanny meetings. You must know that these witches have dreadful appetites, and that there is nothing in the world of which they are so fond as boiled baby.

Ees-tée-ah Muts, who was a very good man, had no suspicion that his wife was guilty of such practices, and she was very careful to keep him in ignorance of it.

One day, when the witch-wife was planning to go to a meeting, she stole a fat young baby and put it to cook in a great olla (earthen jar) in the dark inner room. But before night she found she must go for water, and as the strange stone reservoir at Acoma is a laborious half-mile from the houses, she would be gone some time. So, as she departed with a bright-painted tinaja upon her head, she charged her husband on no account to enter the inner room.

When she was gone Ees-tée-ah Muts began to ponder what she had said, and he feared that all was not well. He went to the inner room and looked around, and when he found the baby cooking he was grieved, as any good husband would be, for then he knew that his wife was a witch. But when his wife returned with water, he said not a word, keeping only a sharp lookout to see what would come.

Very early that night Ees-tée-ah Muts pretended to go to sleep, but he was really very wide awake. His wife was quiet, but he could feel that she was watching him. Presently a cat came sneaking into the room and whispered to the witch-wife:

"Why do you not come to the meeting, for we await you?"

"Wait me yet a little," she whispered, "until the man is sound asleep."

The cat crept away, and Ees-tée-ah Muts kept very still. By and by an owl came in and bade the woman hurry. And at last, thinking her husband asleep, the witch-wife rose noiselessly and went out. As soon as she was gone, Ees-tée-ah Muts got up and followed her at a distance, for it was a night of the full moon.

The witch-wife walked a long way till she came to the foot of the Black Mesa, where was a great dark hole with a rainbow in its mouth. As she passed under the rainbow she turned herself into a cat and disappeared within the cave. Ees-tée-ah Muts crept softly up and peered in. He saw a great firelit room full of witches in the shapes of ravens and vultures, wolves and other animals of ill omen. They were gathered about their feast and were enjoying themselves greatly, eating and dancing and singing and planning evil to mankind.

For a long time Ees-tée-ah Muts watched them, but at last one caught sight of his face peering in at the hole.

"Bring him in!" shouted the chief witch, and many of them rushed out and surrounded him and dragged him into the cave.

"Now," said the chief witch, who was very angry, "we have caught you as a spy and we ought to kill you. But if you will save your life and be one of us, go home and bring me the hearts of your mother and sister, and I will teach you all our ways, so that you shall be a mighty wizard."

Ees-tée-ah Muts hurried home to Acoma and killed two sheep; for he knew, as every Indian knows, that it was useless to try to escape from the witches. Taking the hearts of the sheep, he quickly returned to the chief witch, to whom he gave them. But when the chief witch pricked the hearts with a sharp stick they swelled themselves out like a frog. Then he knew that he had been deceived, and was very angry, but pretending not to care he ordered Ees-tée-ah Muts to go home, which the frightened hunter was very glad to do.

But next morning when Ees-tée-ah Muts awoke he was not in his own home at all, but lying on a tiny shelf far up a dizzy cliff. To jump was certain death, for it was a thousand feet to the ground; and climb he could not, for the smooth rock rose a thousand feet above his head. Then he knew that he had been bewitched by the chief of those that have the evil road, and that he must die. He could hardly move without falling from the narrow shelf, and there he lay with bitter thoughts until the sun was high overhead.

At last a young Squirrel came running along the ledge, and, seeing him, ran back to its mother, crying:

"Nana! Nana! Here is a dead man lying on our ledge!"

"No, he is not dead," said the Squirrel-mother when she had looked, "but I think he is very hungry. Here, take this acorn-cup and carry him some corn-meal and water."

The young Squirrel brought the acorn-cup full of wet corn-meal, but Ees-tée-ah Muts would not take it, for he thought:

"Pah! What is so little when I am fainting for food?"

But the Squirrel-mother, knowing what was in his heart, said:

"Not so, Sau-kée-ne [friend]. It looks to be little, but there will be more than enough. Eat and be strong."

Still doubting, Ees-tée-ah Muts took the cup and ate of the blue corn-meal until he could eat no longer, and yet the acorn-cup was not empty. Then the young Squirrel took the cup and brought it full of water, and though he was very thirsty he could not drain it.

"Now, friend," said the Squirrel-mother, when he was refreshed by his meal, "you cannot yet get down from here, where the witches put you; but wait, for I am the one that will help you."

She went to her store-room and brought out a pine-cone, which she dropped over the great cliff. Ees-tée-ah Muts lay on the narrow ledge as patiently as he could, sleeping sometimes and sometimes thinking of his strange plight. Next morning he could see a stout young pine-tree growing at the bottom of the cliff, where he was very sure there had been no tree at all the day before. Before night it was a large tree, and the second morning it was twice as tall. The young Squirrel brought him meal and water in the acorn-cup twice a day, and now he began to be confident that he would escape.

By the evening of the fourth day the magic pine towered far above his head, and it was so close to the cliff that he could touch it from his shelf.

"Now, Friend Man," said the Squirrel-mother, "follow me!" and she leaped lightly into the tree. Ees-tée-ah Muts seized a branch and swung over into the tree, and letting himself down from bough to bough, at last reached the ground in safety.

The Squirrel-mother came with him to the ground, and he thanked her for her kindness.

"But now I must go back to my home," she said. "Take these seeds of the pine-tree and these piñon-nuts which I have brought for you, and be very careful of them. When you get home, give your wife the pine-seeds, but you must eat the piñons. So now, good-by," and off she went up the tree.

When Ees-tée-ah Muts had come to Acoma and climbed the dizzy stone ladder and stood in the adobe town, he was very much surprised. For the four days of his absence had really been four years, and the people looked strange. All had given him up for dead, and his witch-wife had married another man, but still lived in the same house, which was hers.[1] When Ees-tée-ah Muts entered she seemed very glad to see him, and pretended to know nothing of what had befallen him. He said nothing about it, but talked pleasantly while he munched the piñon-nuts, giving her the pine-seeds to eat. Her new husband made a bed for Ees-tée-ah Muts, and in the morning very early the two men went away together on a hunt.

That afternoon the mother of the witch-wife went to visit her daughter, but when she came near the house she stopped in terror, for far up through the roof grew a great pine-tree, whose furry arms came out at doors and windows. That was the end of the witch-wife, for the magic seed had sprouted in her stomach, and she was turned into a great, sad Pine that swayed above her home, and moaned and sobbed forever, as all her Pine-children do to this day.

---

1.   It is one of the fundamental customs of the Pueblos that the house and its general contents belong to the wife; the fields and other outside property to the husband.

THE DRAIGLIN' HOGNEY

Scotland

There was once a man who had three sons, and very little money to provide for them. So, when the eldest had grown into a lad, and saw that there was no means of making a livelihood at home, he went to his father and said to him: "Father, if thou wilt give me a horse to ride on, a hound to hunt with, and a hawk to fly, I will go out into the wide world and seek my fortune."

His father gave him what he asked for; and he set out on his travels. He rode and he rode, over mountain and glen, until, just at nightfall, he came to a thick, dark wood. He entered it, thinking that he might find a path that would lead him through it; but no path was visible, and after wandering up and down for some time, he was obliged to acknowledge to himself that he was completely lost.

There seemed to be nothing for it but to tie his horse to a tree, and make a bed of leaves for himself on the ground; but just as he was about to do so he saw a light glimmering in the distance, and, riding on in the direction in which it was, he soon came to a clearing in the wood, in which stood a magnificent Castle.

The windows were all lit up, but the great door was barred; and, after he had ridden up to it, and knocked, and received no answer, the young man raised his hunting horn to his lips and blew a loud blast in the hope of letting the inmates know that he was without.

Instantly the door flew open of its own accord, and the young man entered, wondering very much what this strange thing would mean. And he wondered still more when he passed from room to room, and found that, although fires were burning brightly everywhere, and there was a plentiful meal laid out on the table in the great hall, there did not seem to be a single person in the whole of the vast building.

However, as he was cold, and tired, and wet, he put his horse in one of the stalls of the enormous stable, and taking his hawk and hound along with him, went into the hall and ate a hearty supper. After which he sat down by the side of the fire, and began to dry his clothes.

By this time it had grown late, and he was just thinking of retiring to one of the bedrooms which he had seen upstairs and going to bed, when a clock which was hanging on the wall struck twelve.

Instantly the door of the huge apartment opened, and a most awful-looking Draiglin' Hogney entered. His hair was matted and his beard was long, and his eyes shone like stars of fire from under his bushy eyebrows, and in his hands he carried a queerly shaped club.

He did not seem at all astonished to see his unbidden guest; but, coming across the hall, he sat down upon the opposite side of the fireplace, and, resting his chin on his hands, gazed fixedly at him.

"Doth thy horse ever kick any?" he said at last, in a harsh, rough voice.

"Ay, doth he," replied the young man; for the only steed that his father had been able to give him was a wild and unbroken colt.

"I have some skill in taming horses," went on the Draiglin' Hogney, "and I will give thee something to tame thine withal. Throw this over him"—and he pulled one of the long, coarse hairs out of his head and gave it to the young man. And there was something so commanding in the Hogney's voice that he did as he was bid, and went out to the stable and threw the hair over the horse.

Then he returned to the hall, and sat down again by the fire. The moment that he was seated the Draiglin' Hogney asked another question.

"Doth thy hound ever bite any?"

"Ay, verily," answered the youth; for his hound was so fierce-tempered that no man, save his master, dare lay a hand on him.

"I can cure the wildest tempered dog in Christendom," replied the Draiglin' Hogney. "Take that, and throw it over him." And he pulled another hair out of his head and gave it to the young man, who lost no time in flinging it over his hound.

There was still a third question to follow. "Doth ever thy hawk peck any?"

The young man laughed. "I have ever to keep a bandage over her eyes, save when she is ready to fly," said he; "else were nothing safe within her reach."

"Things will be safe now," said the Hogney, grimly. "Throw that over her." And for the third time he pulled a hair from his head and handed it to his companion. And as the other hairs had been thrown over the horse and the hound, so this one was thrown over the hawk.

Then, before the young man could draw breath, the fiercesome Draiglin' Hogney had given him such a clout on the side of his head with his queer-shaped club that he fell down in a heap on the floor.

And very soon his hawk and his hound tumbled down still and motionless beside him; and, out in the stable, his horse became stark and stiff, as if turned to stone. For the Draiglin's words had meant more than at first appeared when he said that he could make all unruly animals quiet.

Some time afterwards the second of the three sons came to his father in the old home with the same request that his brother had made. That he should be provided with a horse, a hawk, and a hound, and be allowed to go out to seek his fortune. And his father listened to him, and gave him what he asked, as he had given his brother.

And the young man set out, and in due time came to the wood, and lost himself in it, just as his brother had done; then he saw the light, and came to the Castle, and went in, and had supper, and dried his clothes, just as it all had happened before.

And the Draiglin' Hogney came in, and asked him the three questions, and he gave the same three answers, and received three hairs—one to throw over his horse, one to throw over his hound, and one to throw over his hawk; then the Hogney killed him, just as he had killed his brother.

Time passed, and the youngest son, finding that his two elder brothers never returned, asked his father for a horse, a hawk, and a hound, in order that he might go and look for them. And the poor old man, who was feeling very desolate in his old age, gladly gave them to him.

So he set out on his quest, and at nightfall he came, as the others had done, to the thick wood and the Castle. But, being a wise and cautious youth, he liked not the way in which he found things. He liked not the empty house; he liked not the spread-out feast; and, most of all, he liked not the look of the Draiglin' Hogney when he saw him. And he determined to be very careful what he said or did as long as he was in his company.

So when the Draiglin' Hogney asked him if his horse kicked, he replied that it did, in very few words; and when he got one of the Hogney's hairs to throw over him, he went out to the stable, and pretended to do so, but he brought it back, hidden in his hand, and, when his unchancy companion was not looking, he threw it into the fire. It fizzled up like a tongue of flame with a little hissing sound like that of a serpent.

"What's that fizzling?" asked the Giant suspiciously.

"'Tis but the sap of the green wood," replied the young man carelessly, as he turned to caress his hound.

The answer satisfied the Draiglin' Hogney, and he paid no heed to the sound which the hair that should have been thrown over the hound, or the sound which the hair that should have been thrown over the hawk, made, when the young man threw them into the fire; and they fizzled up in the same way that the first had done.

Then, thinking that he had the stranger in his power, he whisked across the hearthstone to strike him with his club, as he had struck his brothers; but the young man was on the outlook, and when he saw him coming he gave a shrill whistle. And his horse, which loved him dearly, came galloping in from the stable, and his hound sprang up from the hearthstone where he had been sleeping; and his hawk, who was sitting on his shoulder, ruffled up her feathers and screamed harshly; and they all fell on the Draiglin' Hogney at once, and he found out only too well how the horse kicked, and the hound bit, and the hawk pecked; for they kicked him, and bit him, and pecked him, till he was as dead as a door nail.

When the young man saw that he was dead, he took his little club from his hand, and, armed with that, he set out to explore the Castle.

As he expected, he found that there were dark and dreary dungeons under it, and in one of them he found his two brothers, lying cold and stiff side by side. He touched them with the club, and instantly they came to life again, and sprang to their feet as well as ever.

Then he went into another dungeon; and there were the two horses, and the two hawks, and the two hounds, lying as if dead, exactly as their Masters had lain. He touched them with his magic club, and they, too, came to life again.

Then he called to his two brothers, and the three young men searched the other dungeons, and they found great stores of gold and silver hidden in them, enough to make them rich for life.

So they buried the Draiglin' Hogney, and took possession of the Castle; and two of them went home and brought their old father back with them, and they all were as prosperous and happy as they could be; and, for aught that I know, they are living there still.

THE IRON WOLF

Ukraine

There was once upon a time a parson who had a servant, and when this servant had served him faithfully for twelve years and upward, he came to the parson and said, "Let us now settle our accounts, master, and pay me what thou owest me. I have now served long enough, and would fain have a little place in the wide world all to myself."—"Good!" said the parson. "I'll tell thee now what wage I'll give thee for thy faithful service. I'll give thee this egg. Take it home, and when thou gettest there, make to thyself a cattle-pen, and make it strong; then break the egg in the middle of thy cattle-pen, and thou shalt see something. But whatever thou doest, don't break it on thy way home, or all thy luck will leave thee."

So the servant departed on his homeward way. He went on and on, and at last he thought to himself, "Come now, I'll see what is inside this egg of mine!" So he broke it, and out of it came all sorts of cattle in such numbers that the open steppe became like a fair. The servant stood there in amazement, and he thought to himself, "However in God's world shall I be able to drive all these cattle back again?" He had scarcely uttered the words when the Iron Wolf came running up, and said to him, "I'll collect and drive back all these cattle into the egg again, and I'll patch the egg up so that it will become quite whole. But in return for that," continued the Iron Wolf, "whenever thou dost sit down on the bridal bench,[1]

---

1.   *Posad*, or *posag*, a bench covered with white cloth on which the bride and bridegroom sat down together.

I'll come and eat thee."—"Well," thought the servant to himself, "a lot of things may happen before I sit down on the bridal bench and he comes to eat me, and in the meantime I shall get all these cattle. Agreed, then," said he. So the Iron Wolf immediately collected all the cattle, and drove them back into the egg, and patched up the egg and made it whole just as it was before.

The servant went home to the village where he lived, made him a cattle-pen stronger than strong, went inside it and broke the egg, and immediately that cattle-pen was as full of cattle as it could hold. Then he took to farming and cattle-breeding, and he became so rich that in the whole wide world there was none richer than he. He kept to himself, and his goods increased and multiplied exceedingly; the only thing wanting to his happiness was a wife, but a wife he was afraid to take. Now near to where he lived was a General who had a lovely daughter, and this daughter fell in love with the rich man. So the General went and said to him, "Come, why don't you marry? I'll give you my daughter and lots of money with her."—"How is it possible for me to marry?" replied the man; "as soon as ever I sit down on the bridal bench, the Iron Wolf will come and eat me up." And he told the General all that had happened.—"Oh, nonsense!" said the General, "don't be afraid. I have a mighty host, and when the time comes for you to sit down on the bridal bench, we'll surround your house with three strong rows of soldiers, and they won't let the Iron Wolf get at you, I can tell you." So they talked the matter over till he let himself be persuaded, and then they began to make great preparations for the bridal banquet. Everything went off excellently well, and they made merry till the time came when bride and bridegroom were to sit down together on the bridal bench. Then the General placed his men in three strong rows all round the house so as not to let the Iron Wolf get in; and no sooner had the young people sat down upon the bridal bench, than, sure enough, the Iron Wolf came running up. He saw the host standing round the house in three strong rows, but through all three rows he leaped and made straight for the house. But the man, as soon as he saw the Iron Wolf, leaped out of the window, mounted his horse, and galloped off with the wolf after him.

Away and away he galloped, and after him came the wolf, but try as it would, it could not catch him up anyhow. At last, toward evening, the man stopped and looked about him, and saw that he was in a lone forest, and before him stood a hut. He went up to this hut, and saw an old man and an old woman sitting in front of it, and said to them, "Would you let me rest a little while with you, good people?"—"By all means!" said they.—"There is one thing, however, good people!" said he, "don't let the Iron Wolf catch me while I am resting with you."—"Have no fear of that!" replied the old couple. "We have a dog called Chutko,[2] who can hear a wolf coming a mile off, and he'll be sure to let us know." So he laid him down to sleep, and was just dropping off when Chutko began to bark. Then the old people awoke him, and said, "Be off! be off! for the Iron Wolf is coming." And they gave him the dog, and a wheaten hearth-cake as provision by the way.

So he went on and on, and the dog followed after him till it began to grow dark, and then he perceived another hut in another forest. He went up to that hut, and in front of it were sitting an old man and an old woman. He asked them for a night's lodging. "Only," said he, "take care that the Iron Wolf doesn't catch me!"—"Have no fear of that," said they. "We have a dog here called Vazhko,[3] who can hear a wolf nine miles off." So he laid him down and slept. Just before dawn Vazhko began to bark. Immediately they awoke him. "Run!" cried they, "the Iron Wolf is coming!" And they gave him the dog, and a barley hearth-cake as provision by the way. So he took the hearth-cake, sat him on his horse, and off he went, and his two dogs followed after him.

He went on and on. On and on he went till evening, when again he stopped and looked about him, and he saw that he was in another forest, and another little hut stood before him. He went into the hut, and there were sitting an old man and an old woman. "Will you let me pass the night here, good people?" said he; "only take care that the Iron Wolf does not get hold of me!"—"Have no fear!" said they, "we have a dog called Bary, who can hear a wolf coming twelve miles off. He'll let us know." So he lay down to sleep, and early in the morning Bary let them know that the Iron Wolf was drawing nigh. Immediately they awoke him. "'Tis high time for you to be off!" said they. Then they gave him the dog,

---

2. Hearkener.
3. Heavysides.

and a buckwheat hearth-cake as provision by the way. He took the hearth-cake, sat him on his horse, and off he went. So now he had three dogs, and they all three followed him.

He went on and on, and toward evening he found himself in front of another hut. He went into it, and there was nobody there. He went and lay down, and his dogs lay down also, Chutko on the threshold of the room door, Vazhko at the threshold of the house door, and Bary at the threshold of the outer gate. Presently the Iron Wolf came trotting up. Immediately Chutko gave the alarm, Vazhko nailed him to the earth, and Bary tore him to pieces.

Then the man gathered his faithful dogs around him, mounted his horse, and went back to his own home.

THE YOUNG MAN
WHO WOULD HAVE HIS
EYES OPENED

☼

Estonia

Once upon a time there lived a youth who was never happy unless he was prying into something that other people knew nothing about. After he had learned to understand the language of birds and beasts, he discovered accidentally that a great deal took place under cover of night which mortal eyes never saw. From that moment he felt he could not rest till these hidden secrets were laid bare to him, and he spent his whole time wandering from one wizard to another, begging them to open his eyes, but found none to help him. At length he reached an old magician called Mana, whose learning was greater than that of the rest, and who could tell him all he wanted to know. But when the old man had listened attentively to him, he said, warningly:

"My son, do not follow after empty knowledge, which will not bring you happiness, but rather evil. Much is hidden from the eyes of men, because did they know everything their hearts would no longer be at peace. Knowledge kills joy, therefore think well what you are doing, or some day you will repent. But if you will not take my advice, then truly I can show you the secrets of the night. Only you will need more than a man's courage to bear the sight."

He stopped and looked at the young man, who nodded his head, and then the wizard continued, "To-morrow night you must go to the place where, once in seven years, the serpent-king gives a great feast to his whole court. In front of him stands a golden bowl filled with goats' milk, and if you can manage to dip a piece of bread in this milk, and eat it before you are obliged to fly, you will understand all the secrets of the night that are hidden from other men. It is lucky for you that the serpent-king's feast happens to fall this year, otherwise you would have had long to wait for it. But take care to be quick and bold, or it will be the worse for you."

The young man thanked the wizard for his counsel, and went his way firmly resolved to carry out his purpose, even if he paid for it with his life; and when night came he set out for a wide, lonely moor, where the serpent-king held his feast. With sharpened eyes, he looked eagerly all round him, but could see nothing but a multitude of small hillocks that lay motionless under the moonlight. He crouched behind a bush for some time, till he felt that midnight could not be far off, when suddenly there arose in the middle of the moor a brilliant glow, as if a star was shining over one of the hillocks. At the same moment all the hillocks began to writhe and to crawl, and from each one came hundreds of serpents and made straight for the glow, where they knew they should find their king. When they reached the hillock where he dwelt, which was higher and broader than the rest, and had a bright light hanging over the top, they coiled themselves up and waited. The whirr and confusion from all the serpent-houses were so great that the youth did not dare to advance one step, but remained where he was, watching intently all that went on; but at last he began to take courage, and moved on softly step by step.

What he saw was creepier than creepy, and surpassed all he had ever dreamt of. Thousands of snakes, big and little and of every colour, were gathered together in one great cluster round a huge serpent, whose body was as thick as a beam, and which had on its head a golden crown, from which the light sprang. Their hissings and darting tongues so terrified the young man that his heart sank, and he felt he should never have courage to push on to certain death, when suddenly he caught sight of the golden bowl in front of the serpent-king, and knew that if he lost this chance it would never come back. So, with his hair standing on end and his blood frozen in his veins, he crept forwards. Oh! what a noise and a whirr rose afresh among the serpents. Thousands of heads were reared, and tongues were stretched out to sting the intruder to death, but happily for him their bodies were so closely entwined one in the other that they could not disentangle themselves quickly. Like lightning he seized a bit of bread, dipped it in the bowl, and put it in his mouth, then dashed away as if fire was pursuing him. On he flew as if a whole army of foes were at his heels, and he seemed to hear the noise of their approach growing nearer and nearer. At length his breath failed him, and he threw himself almost senseless on the turf. While he lay there dreadful dreams haunted him. He thought that the serpent-king with the fiery crown had twined himself round him, and was crushing out his life. With a loud shriek he sprang up to do battle with his enemy, when he saw that it was rays of the sun which had wakened him. He rubbed his eyes and looked all round, but nothing could he see of the foes of the past night, and the moor where he had run into such danger must be at least a mile away. But it was no dream that he had run hard and far, or that he had drunk of the magic goats' milk. And when he felt his limbs, and found them whole, his joy was great that he had come through such perils with a sound skin.

After the fatigues and terrors of the night, he lay still till mid-day, but he made up his mind he would go that very evening into the forest to try what the goats' milk could really do for him, and if he would now be able to understand all that had been a mystery to him. And once in the forest his doubts were set at rest, for he saw what no mortal eyes had ever seen before. Beneath the trees were golden pavilions, with flags of silver all brightly lighted up. He was still wondering why the pavilions were there, when a noise was heard among the trees, as if the wind had suddenly got up, and on all sides beautiful maidens stepped from the trees into the bright light of the moon. These were the wood-nymphs, daughters of the earth-mother, who came every night to hold their dances, in the forest. The young man, watching from his hiding place, wished he had a hundred eyes in his head, for two were not nearly enough for the sight before him, the dances lasting till the first streaks of dawn. Then a silvery veil seemed to be drawn over the ladies, and they vanished from sight. But the young man remained where he was till the sun was high in the heavens, and then went home.

He felt that day to be endless, and counted the minutes till night should come, and he might return to the forest. But when at last he got there he found neither pavilions nor nymphs, and though he went back many nights after he never saw them again. Still, he thought about them night and day, and ceased to care about anything else in the world, and was sick to the end of his life with longing for that beautiful vision. And that was the way he learned that the wizard had spoken truly when he said, "Blindness is man's highest good."

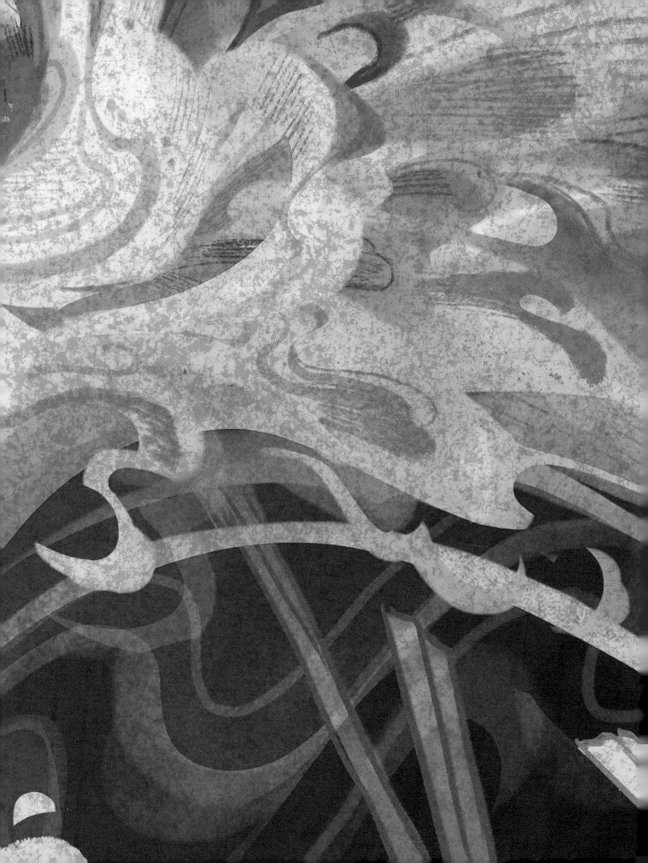

Over Water,
Under Water

THE MAN-WHALE

Iceland

In ancient times, in the south part of the country, it was the custom to go in a boat, at a certain season of the year, from the mainland to the cliffs, Geirfuglasker, to procure sea-birds and the eggs which they were in the habit of laying there. The passage to these rocks was always looked upon as an unsafe one, as they stood some way out at sea, and a constant and heavy surf beat upon them.

It happened once that some men went thither in a boat at the proper season for the purpose, as the weather seemed to promise a long calm. When they arrived at the rocks, some of them landed, the rest being left to take care of the boat. Suddenly a heavy wind came on, and the latter were forced to leave the island in haste, as the sea became dangerous and the surf beat furiously upon the cliffs. All those who had landed were enabled to reach the boat in time, at the signal from their companions, except one, a young and active man, who, having gone in his zeal higher and farther than the others, was longer in getting down to the beach again. By the time he did get down, the waves were so high, that though those in the boat wrought their best to save him, they could not get near enough to him, and so were compelled for their own lives' sake to row to shore. They determined, however, when the storm should abate its fury, to return to the rocks and rescue him, knowing that unless they did so and the wind were soon spent, the youth could not but perish from cold and hunger. Often they tried to row to the Geirfuglasker, but, the whole season through, they were unable to approach them, as the wind and surf always drove them back. At last, deeming the young man dead, they gave up the attempt and ceased to risk their lives in seas so wrathful.

So time passed away, until the next season for seeking sea-birds came round, and the weather being now calm, the peasants embarked in their boat for the Geirfuglasker. When they landed upon the cliffs, great was their astonishment at seeing come towards them a man, for they thought that no one could live in so wild and waste a spot. When the man drew near them, and they recognized him as the youth who had been left there the year before, and whom they had long ago given up as lost, their wonder knew no bounds, and they guessed that he had the elves to thank for his safety. They asked him all sorts of questions. What had he lived upon? Where had he slept at night? What had he done for fire in the winter? and so forth, but he would give them none but vague replies, which left them just as wise as they were before. He said, however, he had never once left the cliff, and that he had been very comfortable there, wanting for nothing. They then rowed him to land, where all his friends and kin received him with unbounded amazement and joy, but, question him as they would, could get but mighty little out of him concerning his life on the cliffs the whole year through. With time, the strangeness of this event and the wonder it had awakened passed away from men's minds, and it was little if at all more spoken of.

One Sunday in the summer, certain things that took place in the church at Hvalsnes filled people with astonishment. There were large numbers there, and among them the young man who had passed a year on the cliffs of the Geirfuglasker. When the service was over and the folk began to leave the church, what should they find standing in the porch but a beautiful cradle with a baby in it. The coverlet was richly embroidered, and wrought of a stuff that nobody had ever seen before. But the strangest part of the business was, that though everybody looked at the cradle and child, nobody claimed either one or the other, or seemed to know anything whatever about them. Last of all came the priest out of church, who, after he had admired and wondered at the cradle and child as much as the others, asked whether there was no one present to whom they belonged. No one answered. Then he asked whether there was no one present who had enough interest in the child to desire him to baptize it. No one either answered or came forward.

At this moment the priest happened to cast his eyes on the young peasant, concerning whose sojourn on the Geirfuglasker rocks he had always felt particularly suspicious, and calling him aside, asked him whether he had any idea who its father was, and whether he would like the child baptized. But the youth turning angrily from him declared that he knew nothing whatever about the child or its father.

"What care I," he said, "whether you baptize the child or no? Christen it or drown it, just which you think fit; neither it, nor its father, nor its mother, are aught to me."

As these words left his lips, there suddenly appeared in the porch a woman, handsomely apparelled, of great beauty and noble stature, whom no one had ever seen before. She snatched the coverlet from the cradle, and flinging it in through the door of the church, said:

"Be witnesses all, that I wish not the church to lose its dues for this child's baptism."

Then turning to the young peasant, and stretching out her hands towards him she cried, "But thou, faithless coward, disowner of thy child, shalt become a whale, the fiercest and most dreaded in the whole wide sea!"

With these words, she seized the cradle and disappeared.

The priest, however, took the coverlet which she had flung into the church, and made of it an altar-cloth, the handsomest that had ever been seen. As for the young peasant, he went mad on the spot; and, rushing down to the Holmur Cliffs, which rise sheer from the deep water, made as if he would throw himself from them. But while he hesitated for a moment on the brink, lo! a fearful change came over him, and he began to swell to a vast size, till, at last, he became so large, that the rock could no longer bear him, but crumbling beneath him hurled him into the sea. There he was changed into a great whale, and the red cap which he had been wearing became a red head.

After this, his mother confessed that her son had spent the year with the elves upon the Geirfuglasker. On his being left on the rocks by his companions (so he had declared to her), he had at first wandered about in despair, filled only with the thought of throwing himself into the waves to die a speedy death rather than suffer all the pangs of hunger and cold; but a lovely girl had come to him, and telling him she was an elf, had asked him to spend the winter with her. She had borne him a child before the end of the year, and only allowed him to go to shore when his companions came again to the cliffs, on condition that he would have this child baptized when he should find it in the church-porch, threatening him, if he failed in the fulfilment of this, with the severest punishment and most hapless fate.

Now Redhead, the whale, took up his abode in the Faxafjörd, and wrought mischief there without end, destroying boats innumerable, and drowning all their crews, so that at last it became unsafe to cross any part of the bay, and nothing could either prevent his ravages or drive him away. After matters had gone on like this for some time, the whale began to haunt a narrow gulf between Akranes and Kjarlarnes, which is now called after him, Hvalfjördur.

At that time there lived at Saurboer, in Hvalfjardarströnd, an aged priest, who, though hale and hearty, was blind. He had two sons and a daughter, who were all in the flower of their youth, and who were their father's hope and stay, and, as it were, the very apple of his eye. His sons were in the habit of fishing in Hvalfjördur, and one day when they were out they encountered the whale, Redhead, who overthrew their boat and drowned them both. When their father heard of their death, and how it had been brought about, he was filled with grief but uttered not a word at the time.

Now it must be known that this old priest was well skilled in all magical arts.

Not long after this, one fine morning in the summer, he bade his daughter take his hand and guide him down to the sea-shore. When he arrived there, he planted the end of the staff which he had brought with him, in the waves, and leaning on the handle fell into deep thought.

After a few minutes he asked his daughter, "How looks the sea?"

She answered, "My father, it is as bright and smooth as a mirror."

Again, a few minutes, and he repeated, "How looks the sea?"

She replied, "I see on the horizon a black line, which draws nearer and nearer, as it were a shoal of whales, swimming quickly into the bay."

When the old man heard that the black line was approaching them, he bade the girl lead him along the shore towards the inland end of the bay. She did so, and the black surging sea followed them constantly. But as the water became shallower, the girl saw that the foam arose, not from a shoal of whales, as she had thought at first, but from the swimming of a single huge whale with a red head, who came rapidly towards them along the middle of the bay, as if drawn to them by some unseen power. A river ran into the extreme end of the gulf, and the old priest begged his daughter to lead him still on along its banks. As they went slowly up the stream, the old man feeling every footstep before him, the whale followed them, though with a heavy struggle, as the river contained but little water for so vast a monster to swim in. Yet forward they went, and the whale still after them, till the river became so narrow between its high walls of rock, that the ground beneath their feet quaked as the whale followed them. After a while they came to a waterfall, up which the monster leaped with a spring that made the land tremble far and wide, and the very rocks totter. But they came at last to a lake, from which the river rose, whose course they had followed from the sea; the lake Hvalvatn. Here the heart of the monster broke from very toil and anguish, and he disappeared from their eyes.

When the old priest returned home, after having charmed the whale thus to his death, all the people from far and near thanked him for having rid their coasts of so dread a plague.

And in case anybody should doubt the truth of this story of Redhead, the man-whale, we may as well say that on the shores of the lake Hvalvatn, mighty whale-bones were found lying long after the date of this tale.

NYA-NYA BULEMBU; or,
the MOSS-GREEN PRINCESS:
a SWAZI TALE

✿

South Africa

There was once a little Princess named Kitila, the prettiest and nicest child you could possibly find. She was her mother's one delight, and her father was a very great Chief indeed. But for all that many little girls were far happier than she, for her father hated her mother and did everything he could to show how much he despised her and her child. He did not allow Kitila so much as one necklace of beads, and her little skin cloak was shabby and poor. He had another daughter, Mapindane, whose mother was his favourite Queen. He loved her dearly, and delighted in her beauty and pretty ways, for she also was a charming child. But so much did he dislike Kitila that he was quite annoyed to see that she was pretty and likely to be admired.

At last he determined to humiliate her and her mother for ever by dressing her in the skin of the Nya-nya Bulembu, so that every one might be frightened of her and no Prince might ever love her.

Now the Nya-nya Bulembu is a strange beast who lives in the water. He has long teeth and claws, and his skin is covered with bright green moss. No one has anything to do with him who can help it, and his very name means "the Despised One covered with Moss." The King thus hoped that his little girl would be taken for the monster himself, and would be hated by all as much as he himself disliked her. You will see, however, that he would have done much better to be kind to his little daughter, for the Nya-nya Bulembu is a fairy beast, and it is not wise to meddle with him.

One day the King called his Chief Councillors and his people together and told them of his intentions. "The little Princess Kitila," he said, "is to be dressed in the skin of the Nya-nya Bulembu. Fetch me an animal which is young, with regular teeth, long claws, and a perfect skin well covered with green moss."

The King also gave orders for plenty of green mealie-bread to be made with which to entice the animal out of the water. A party of picked men then went out together and came down to the river. They followed its course till they came to a deep pool, where the water was quite black. The huntsmen stood round in a ring and sang the song of the Nya-nya Bulembu:

"Nya-nya Bulembu, Nya-nya Bulembu,
Come out of the water and eat me!
The King has sent us for the great Nya-nya Bulembu!
Come and let us see you!
Laugh and show us your teeth!"

Out came a huge old monster, with only two or three teeth left, and no moss on his skin at all.

"No," said the huntsmen at once, "we don't want you."

They journeyed on again in a great storm of wind and rain. When it had passed away, and the sun shone once more, they found themselves at a second big pool, which was blue as the sky. Here they stopped and sang the song of the Bulembu once more. Out came a vicious-looking creature, with but little moss on his coat, and only one tooth three feet long.

"No, we don't want you either," said the huntsmen, and they travelled on again till they came to a third pool, which was bright green. Round it grew a most beautiful fringe of green moss, and the water itself was vivid green, like the grass in spring.

Once more the huntsmen sang the magic song, and out came a nice green Bulembu, beautifully covered with moss, and showing all his long white teeth. They set big pieces of mealie-bread for him, and as he came out to eat they caught him alive. Then they travelled like the wind to the King's kraal. As they drew near home they sang:

"Have all your assegais ready!
The Nya-nya Bulembu is coming!"

All the men in the kraal seized their assegais and hurried to the gate by which the Bulembu must enter. They stood in line in front of the entrance, and as the green monster rushed upon them he fell on their spears and died. Then they took the body to the hut of the despised Queen, and began to prepare the skin for use.

First they cut the body open, and to their great surprise out came the most lovely bead-work. There were necklaces, bracelets, and girdles of every colour and pattern, the most lovely little embroidered bags, and the most beautifully woven mats. Nothing that a King's daughter could want was missing, and everything was of the finest workmanship. It seemed as if the supply would never come to an end, for the more beads they pulled out the more appeared, till there were enough to last the Princess her life long. But the moment they began to remove the skin no more appeared. They stripped the Bulembu most carefully, preserving the nails and all the teeth, and when the skin was quite complete they wrapped the little Princess in it. The instant it touched her it fitted as if it were a part of her; indeed, she could not get it off again, for it was the skin of a fairy beast, as the old King knew well. You could no longer see that she was a little girl at all, she looked just like a hideous green monster.

Kitila and her mother cried most bitterly at this undeserved disgrace, but the Chief Councillor could only say, "It is the King's order; we must obey him."

The two little Princesses were never allowed to play with the other children. They sat by themselves every day in the middle of the huts near the cattle-kraal, the one in her green skin with long white teeth, the other in all the prettiest beads imaginable and a lovely little cloak of leopard-skin, the finest the King could procure. The two little girls were great friends, and as they played and ate their food hundreds of little birds came every day and picked up the fragments.

Many years passed by, and the girls grew into womanhood. Mapindane was now very lovely, and was a joy to behold as she sat in the sun, but poor Kitila was still clothed in her hideous green skin, and looked the same as ever. The feast of the first-fruits was now at hand. The King's wise men had been absent a month travelling to the coast to fetch water from the great sea, for no other may be used for the potion which cleanses the land from all evil. They set their calabashes in the sand at low tide, and when they are filled by the magic power of the ocean they return home joyfully. Every day they were expected, and when at last they arrived the King gave orders that all preparations should be made.

The day before the feast every one went out to gather the first-fruits in the fields, and no one remained in the kraal but one old Queen to watch over the two Princesses. The two girls sat in their usual place, and the birds flew round them as they ate and picked up all they could. Suddenly a flock of rock-pigeons swooped down upon them, and in a moment they had seized the beautiful Princess and carried her away, but the green monster they left alone.

The old Queen looked up and shrieked, "There goes the lovely Princess! There goes the King's favourite child!" She called out all the people from the fields and sent them after the pigeons. But the birds rose high into the air, and then headed straight for the North. They carried Mapindane far far away to a new country, and placed her in the kraal of a very great King. There she stayed till the King saw her, and made her his wife, and there she lived in great happiness. But she could never send a message home, for no one had even heard the name of her people, or knew the way through the thick forests which lay between them.

So her father and mother never knew of her good fortune, and always believed that the birds had eaten her. Poor Kitila in her green skin was worse off than ever, for the bereaved Queen was very jealous and angry, and as she was all-powerful, Kitila was no longer allowed to live as a Princess, but was set to do all sorts of degrading work. At last the King said to her, "You are no good at all; you must go and scare birds. You are so ugly that every bird who sees you will fly away at once."

From that day the Princess was no longer called Kitila, but Nya-nya Bulembu. She often said to her mother, "How hard my life is! Why was I born to all this?" But her mother always remembered the Bulembu's magic gifts, and said, "Do not despair; all will come right presently."

And so it did; for the first time the Princess went to the fields she met a Fairy in the shape of a very old man. He took pity on her, and gave her a stick, saying, "When you come to the fields just wave this, and call aloud. All the birds will fall down dead at once. When you go bathing take the stick with you into the water; it will give you your true shape again. But remember never to leave go of it, or your power will depart."

Kitila took the stick, and found it quite as powerful as the Fairy declared. She had no trouble with the birds, but kept the crops in safety as easily as possible. Every day in the hot, still afternoon, when all creatures are asleep, she went down to the river. As her foot touched the water the green skin floated away, and hundreds of pretty girls came to play with her at her call.

She stood in the water and sang:

"Nya-nya Bulembu, Nya-nya Bulembu,
Here I am!
I was dressed like a monster,
But I am like any girl.
To-day they fed me with the dogs."

Then she called for food, and instantly a feast appeared, and she and all the Fairies ate and laughed together. But when she came out of the river her green skin reappeared, and she was once more Nya-nya Bulembu.

The other little boys and girls who were also scaring birds were dreadfully afraid of the monster, and never went near her. They never asked her to join them in the afternoons when they played together in the water, but they often wondered what she looked like when she bathed by herself in a lonely pool. One day they went down to see, but they hid behind the trees, so that the Princess never knew. When a beautiful girl appeared instead of the ugly monster, they were so astonished that they ran straight home and told the whole story to the Princess's mother. The despised Queen was very pleased, but she told the children not to say a word to any one. So the moss-green Princess continued to scare the birds.

Some months later a great Prince came to visit the King. He was young and handsome, but he was noted above all for his wisdom and good judgment. His father had sent him to seek a bride; she was to be the most beautiful woman he could find, and every one was anxious to see the girl chosen by so wise a Prince. The young man travelled far and wide, but found no maiden whom he could love. At last he came to the kraal in which lived the moss-green Princess. He went straight to the King and asked him if he had any daughters.

"Yes," said the King," but I have only one. You shall see her with pleasure."

"Let the Prince see the monster," said Mapindane's mother, with a bitter laugh. So the Prince was taken to the fields where Kitila was scaring birds. When he got there the little boys and girls who were at work came to him and said, "Do you want to see Nya-nya Bulembu? She is bathing just now, we will take you to the pool she always visits."

They took the Prince, and placed him where he could see the moss-green Princess enter the water without being seen by her. When he first saw the green monster appear he held his breath with horror, and thought some trick had been played upon him. But directly this hideous creature touched the water the green skin fell away, and there stood the loveliest maiden he had ever beheld. He instantly fell in love with her, and vowed to make her his wife, no matter what spell might have fallen on her. He watched her all the afternoon playing with the Fairies in the cool green shadows, and longed to join them, but did not dare. He heard Kitila sing the story of her life. Then he went straight back to the kraal and asked to see the King.

"I will marry your monster," he said.

The King was surprised beyond measure, but he consented, and all preparations were made for the wedding. The wonderful presents the green monster had brought years before were now gathered together and made a royal outfit for the young Princess. The Prince returned to his father, and sent a present of one hundred cows to the King, to show in what consideration he held the bride, and also a fine head of cattle for her mother.

Then he waited for the moss-green Princess to come to him, for in Kafir-land the marriage always takes place in the bridegroom's home. All his people waited, too, in great expectation, for the Prince was known to have chosen the most beautiful girl he could find. Their horror was great when they saw a strange green monster arrive, with long white teeth and claws, attended by four bridesmaids.

"What!" said they. "Is this the peerless beauty chosen by so wise a Prince? How can he marry such a monster?"

The poor Princess sat at the door of the chief hut, trembling lest she should be refused admittance, and the Prince repent of so bad a bargain. But he kept faith with her in spite of her green skin, and received her kindly. She was taken to a beautiful hut, and the next day was fixed for the wedding.

Very early in the morning the Princess and her maids went down to a deep pool in the river to bathe. The sun had barely risen, the air was fresh and cool. Nya-nya Bulembu took the stick in her hand and stepped into the water. As she touched it the green skin fell away, but instead of floating on the water it flew straight up into the air, and was carried many miles, till it fell down right at the door of her mother's hut. Then the despised Queen knew that all was well, and her daughter happy at last.

The Princess came out of the water in her true form—no longer Nya-nya Bulembu, but Kitila, the King's daughter. She returned to the kraal with her bridesmaids, all in their wedding array, and was met by the women who were to be her friends in her new home, for they were to take her to the Prince. Great was their joy and astonishment when they saw so lovely a Princess. They declared that such beauty had never been seen among them before, and praised the wisdom of the Prince who had chosen her.

The marriage ceremony then took place, and the Princess lived among them ever after in much happiness and honour. The fame of her beauty was such that people came from South, East, and West to see so lovely a woman.

But the old King was well punished, for while he often heard of the happiness of Nya-nya Bulembu, he never saw his favourite daughter again, and always believed her dead.

THE MERMAID'S LAKE

Guyana

There was a captain of Indians who was also a Piai priest and doctor. He lived on a savanna. His little daughter went down to the river every day to bathe, and was frequently seen splashing, diving, and swimming with a companion of apparently her own age. Much notice was not taken of her doings, as she was a spoilt and wayward child, and allowed by her fond father to do, and to go, whatever and wherever she liked. But one day she was missing.

Evening came, and the captain's daughter was not at home. Search was made for her in the river, but without success. At night the piaiman's wailing was heard supplicating the spirits of the river and savanna to inspire him with the knowledge of his daughter's fate. At the dawn of day he went down to the river and searched about the bank, rattling his goubi-shak-shak, or magic gourd, as it is indiscriminately called (but properly, as by themselves, eumaraca), and chanting in plaintive and sorrowful tones.

At times he would place his ears to the ground and shake his eumaraca, and listen as if seeking to discover by sound a hollow space under ground—a passage from the river. Thus he went on, forming for himself an irregular path upward to the savanna, until he came to the lake. Here he sat down, and in sweetest tones implored for the restitution of his child. There was a motion in the water, and then appeared a mintje mama, mermaid, or merman (Guiana legends tend to the belief of the hermaphrodite nature of these mysterious and fabulous creatures), who laughed derisively and tauntingly while swimming about and lashing the water with his tail. Arrow after arrow, with unerring aim, sped from the captain's bow.

The merman's head and breast were covered with them. He sank down into the lake. But his descent was for a moment only. He returned, and with him the captain's daughter swimming around and plucking out the arrows from the head and breast of her mysterious lover. The captain, tantalised and enraged beyond forbearance at this explicit sign of his daughter's unnatural affection, plunged into the pond with his uplifted cutlass, slashing right and left. A terrible commotion ensued, the water everywhere bubbled and foamed. But the captain has never been seen from that day.

In the bright moonlight nights an occasional Indian traveller passing by, and ignorant of the legend, has heard a woman's voice lamenting. It is the voice of the captain's daughter chanting the death song for her father's memory. In the dry season, when the lake is almost dry, they say that the merman and his Indian wife have retired to the river, and drawn the water after them.

KIVIUNG

Inuit Nunangat

An old woman lived with her grandson in a small hut. As she had no husband and no son to take care of her and the boy, they were very poor, the boy's clothing being made of skins of birds which they caught in snares. When the boy would come out of the hut and join his playfellows, the men would laugh at him and tear his outer garment. Only one man, whose name was Kiviung, was kind to the young boy; but he could not protect him from the others. Often the lad came to his grandmother crying and weeping, and she always consoled him and each time made him a new garment. She entreated the men to stop teasing the boy and tearing his clothing, but they would not listen to her prayer. At last she got angry and swore she would take revenge upon his abusers, and she could easily do so, as she was a great angakoq.

She commanded her grandson to step into a puddle which was on the floor of the hut, telling him what would happen and how he should behave. As soon as he stood in the water the earth opened and he sank out of sight, but the next moment he rose near the beach as a yearling seal with a beautiful skin and swam about lustily.

The men had barely seen the seal when they took to their kayaks, eager to secure the pretty animal. But the transformed boy quickly swam away, as his grandmother had told him, and the men continued in pursuit. Whenever he rose to breathe he took care to come up behind the kayaks, where the men could not get at him with their harpoons; there, however, he splashed and dabbled in order to attract their attention and lure them on. But before any one could turn his kayak he had dived again and swam away. The men were so interested in the pursuit that they did not observe that they were being led far from the coast and that the land was now altogether invisible.

Suddenly a gale arose; the sea foamed and roared and the waves destroyed or upset their frail vessels. After all seemed to be drowned the seal was again transformed into the lad, who went home without wetting his feet. There was nobody now to tear his clothing, all his abusers being dead.

Only Kiviung, who was a great angakoq and had never abused the boy, had escaped the wind and waves. Bravely he strove against the wild sea, but the storm did not abate. After he had drifted for many days on the wide sea, a dark mass loomed up through the mist. His hope revived and he worked hard to reach the supposed land. The nearer he came, however, the more agitated did the sea become, and he saw that he had mistaken a wild, black sea, with raging whirlpools, for land. Barely escaping he drifted again for many days, but the storm did not abate and he did not see any land. Again he saw a dark mass looming up through the mist, but he was once more deceived, for it was another whirlpool which made the sea rise in gigantic waves.

At last the storm moderated, the sea subsided, and at a great distance he saw the land. Gradually he came nearer and following the coast he at length spied a stone house in which a light was burning. He landed and entered the house. Nobody was inside but an old woman whose name was Arnaitiang. She received him kindly and at his request pulled off his boots, slippers, and stockings and dried them on the frame hanging over the lamp. Then she went out to light a fire and cook a good meal.

When the stockings were dry, Kiviung tried to take them from the frame in order to put them on, but as soon as he extended his hand to touch them the frame rose out of his reach. Having tried several times in vain, he called Arnaitiang and asked her to give him back the stockings. She answered: "Take them yourself; there they are; there they are" and went out again. The fact is she was a very bad woman and wanted to eat Kiviung.

Then he tried once more to take hold of his stockings, but with no better result. He called again for Arnaitiang and asked her to give him the boots and stockings, whereupon she said: "Sit down where I sat when you entered my house; then you can get them." After that she left him again. Kiviung tried it once more, but the frame rose as before and he could not reach it.

Now he understood that Arnaitiang meditated mischief; so he summoned his tornaq, a huge white bear, who arose roaring from under the floor of the house. At first Arnaitiang did not hear him, but as Kiviung kept on conjuring the spirit came nearer and nearer to the surface, and when she heard his loud roar she rushed in trembling with fear and gave Kiviung what he had asked for. "Here are your boots," she cried; "here are your slippers; here are your stockings. I'll help you put them on." But Kiviung would not stay any longer with this horrid witch and did not even dare to put on his boots, but took them from Arnaitiang and rushed out of the door. He had barely escaped when it clapped violently together and just caught the tail of his jacket, which was torn off. He hastened to his kayak without once stopping to look behind and paddled away. He had only gone a short distance before Arnaitiang, who had recovered from her fear, came out swinging her glittering woman's knife and threatening to kill him. He was nearly frightened to death and almost upset his kayak. However, he managed to balance it again and cried in answer, lifting up his spear: "I shall kill you with my spear." When Arnaitiang heard these words she fell down terror stricken and broke her knife. Kiviung then observed that it was made of a thin slab of fresh water ice.

He traveled on for many days and nights, following the shore. At last he came to a hut, and again a lamp was burning inside. As his clothing was wet and he was hungry, he landed and entered the house. There he found a woman who lived all alone with her daughter. Her son-in-law was a log of driftwood which had four boughs. Every day about the time of low water they carried it to the beach and when the tide came in it swam away. When night came again it returned with eight large seals, two being fastened to every bough. Thus the timber provided its wife, her mother, and Kiviung with an abundance of food. One day, however, after they had launched it as they had always done, it left and never returned.

After a short interval Kiviung married the young widow. Now he went sealing every day himself and was very successful. As he thought of leaving some day, he was anxious to get a good stock of mittens (that his hands might keep dry during the long journey?). Every night after returning from hunting he pretended to have lost his mittens. In reality he had concealed them in the hood of his jacket.

After awhile the old woman became jealous of her daughter, for the new husband of the latter was a splendid hunter and she wished to marry him herself. One day when he was away hunting, she murdered her daughter, and in order to deceive him she removed her daughter's skin and crept into it, thus changing her shape into that of the young woman. When Kiviung returned, she went to meet him, as it had been her daughter's custom, and without exciting any suspicion. But when he entered the hut and saw the bones of his wife he at once became aware of the cruel deed and of the deception that had been practiced and fled away.

He traveled on for many days and nights, always following the shore. At last he again came to a hut where a lamp was burning. As his clothing was wet and he was hungry, he landed and went up to the house. Before entering it occurred to him that it would be best to find out first who was inside. He therefore climbed up to the window and looked through the peep hole. On the bed sat an old woman, whose name was Aissivang (spider). When she saw the dark figure before the window she believed it was a cloud passing the sun, and as the light was insufficient to enable her to go on with her work she got angry. With her knife she cut away her eyebrows, ate them, and did not mind the dripping blood, but sewed on. When Kiviung saw this he thought that she must be a very bad woman and turned away.

Still he traveled on days and nights. At last he came to a land which seemed familiar to him and soon he recognized his own country. He was very glad when he saw some boats coming to meet him. They had been on a whaling excursion and were towing a great carcass to the village. In the bow of one of them stood a stout young man who had killed the whale. He was Kiviung's son, whom he had left a small boy and who was now grown up and had become a great hunter. His wife had taken a new husband, but now she returned to Kiviung.

THE GOBLIN PONY

France

"Don't stir from the fireplace to-night," said old Peggy, "for the wind is blowing so violently that the house shakes; besides, this is Hallow-e'en, when the witches are abroad, and the goblins, who are their servants, are wandering about in all sorts of disguises, doing harm to the children of men."

"Why should I stay here?" said the eldest of the young people. "No, I must go and see what the daughter of old Jacob, the rope-maker, is doing. She wouldn't close her blue eyes all night if I didn't visit her father before the moon had gone down."

"I must go and catch lobsters and crabs," said the second, "and not all the witches and goblins in the world shall hinder me."

So they all determined to go on their business or pleasure, and scorned the wise advice of old Peggy. Only the youngest child hesitated a minute, when she said to him, "You stay here, my little Richard, and I will tell you beautiful stories."

But he wanted to pick a bunch of wild thyme and some blackberries by moonlight, and ran out after the others. When they got outside the house they said: "The old woman talks of wind and storm, but never was the weather finer or the sky more clear; see how majestically the moon stalks through the transparent clouds!"

Then all of a sudden they noticed a little black pony close beside them.

"Oh, ho!" they said, "that is old Valentine's pony; it must have escaped from its stable, and is going down to drink at the horse-pond."

"My pretty little pony," said the eldest, patting the creature with his hand, "you mustn't run too far; I'll take you to the pond myself."

With these words he jumped on the pony's back and was quickly followed by his second brother, then by the third, and so on, till at last they were all astride the little beast, down to the small Richard, who didn't like to be left behind.

On the way to the pond they met several of their companions, and they invited them all to mount the pony, which they did, and the little creature did not seem to mind the extra weight, but trotted merrily along.

The quicker it trotted the more the young people enjoyed the fun; they dug their heels into the pony's sides and called out, "Gallop, little horse, you have never had such brave riders on your back before!"

In the meantime the wind had risen again, and the waves began to howl; but the pony did not seem to mind the noise, and instead of going to the pond, cantered gaily towards the sea-shore.

Richard began to regret his thyme and blackberries, and the eldest brother seized the pony by the mane and tried to make it turn round, for he remembered the blue eyes of Jacob the rope-maker's daughter. But he tugged and pulled in vain, for the pony galloped straight on into the sea, till the waves met its fore-feet. As soon as it felt the water it neighed lustily and capered about with glee, advancing quickly into the foaming billows. When the waves had covered the children's legs they repented their careless behaviour, and cried out: "The cursed little black pony is bewitched. If we had only listened to old Peggy's advice we shouldn't have been lost."

The further the pony advanced, the higher rose the sea; at last the waves covered the children's heads and they were all drowned.

Towards morning old Peggy went out, for she was anxious about the fate of her grandchildren. She sought them high and low, but could not find them anywhere. She asked all the neighbours if they had seen the children, but no one knew anything about them, except that the eldest had not been with the blue-eyed daughter of Jacob the rope-maker.

As she was going home, bowed with grief, she saw a little black pony coming towards her, springing and curveting in every direction. When it got quite near her it neighed loudly, and galloped past her so quickly that in a moment it was out of her sight.

THE THREE CHESTS:
THE STORY of the WICKED
OLD MAN of the SEA

Finland

There was once an honest old farmer who had three daughters. His farm ran down to the shores of a deep lake. One day as he leaned over the water to take a drink, wicked old Wetehinen reached up from the bottom of the lake and clutched him by the beard.

"Ouch! Ouch!" the farmer cried. "Let me go!"

Wetehinen only held on more tightly.

"Yes, I'll let you go," he said, "but only on this condition: that you give me one of your daughters for wife!"

"Give you one of my daughters? Never!"

"Very well, then I'll never let go!" wicked old Wetehinen declared and with that he began jerking at the beard as if it were a bellrope.

"Wait! Wait!" the farmer spluttered.

Now he didn't want to give one of his daughters to wicked old Wetehinen—of course not! But at the same time he was in Wetehinen's power and he realized that if he didn't do what the old reprobate demanded he might lose his life and so leave all three of his daughters orphans. Perhaps for the good of all he had better sacrifice one of them.

"All right," he said, "let me go and I'll send you my oldest daughter. I promise."

So Wetehinen let go his beard and the farmer scrambled to his feet and hurried home.

"My dear," he said to his oldest daughter, "I left a bit of the harness down at the lake. Like a good girl will you run down and get it for me."

The eldest daughter went at once and when she reached the water's edge, old Wetehinen reached up and caught her about the waist and carried her down to the bottom of the lake where he lived in a big house.

At first he was kind to her. He made her mistress of the house and gave her the keys to all the rooms and closets. He went very carefully over the keys and pointing to one he said:

"That key you must never use for it opens the door to a room which I forbid you to enter."

The eldest daughter began keeping house for old Wetehinen and spent her time cooking and cleaning and spinning much as she used to at home with her father. The days went by and she grew familiar with the house and began to know what was in every room and every closet.

At first she felt no temptation to open the forbidden door. If old Wetehinen wanted to have a secret room, well and good. But why in the world had he given her the key if he really didn't want her to open the door? The more she thought about it the more she wondered. Every time she passed the room she stopped a moment and stared at the door. It looked just exactly like the doors that led into all the other rooms.

"I wonder why he doesn't want me to open just that door?" she kept asking herself.

Finally one day when old Wetehinen was away she thought:

"I don't believe it would matter if I opened that door just a little crack and peeped in once! No one would know the difference!"

For a few moments she hesitated, then mustered up courage enough to turn the key in the forbidden lock and throw open the door.

The room was a storeroom with boxes and chests and old jars piled up around the wall. That was unexciting enough, but in the middle of the floor was something that made her start when she saw what it was. It was blood—that's what it was, a pool of dark red blood! She was about to slam the door shut when she saw something else that made her pause. This was a lovely shining ring that lay in the midst of the pool.

"Oh!" she thought to herself, "what a beautiful ring! If I had it I'd wear it on my finger!"

The longer she looked at it, the more she wanted it.

"If I'm very careful," she said, "I know I could reach over and pick it up without touching the blood."

She tiptoed cautiously into the room, wrapped her skirts tightly about her legs, knelt down on the floor, and stretched her arm over the pool. She picked up the ring very carefully but even so she got a few drops of blood on her fingers.

"No matter!" she thought, "I can wash that off! And see the lovely ring!"

But later, after she had the door again locked, when she tried to wash the blood off, she found she couldn't. She tried soap, she tried sand, she tried everything she could think of, but without success.

"I don't care!" she thought to herself. "If Wetehinen sees the blood, I'll just tell him I cut my finger by accident."

So when Wetehinen came home, she hid the ring and pretended nothing was the matter.

After supper Wetehinen put his head in her lap and said:

"Now, my dear, scratch my head and make me drowsy for bed."

She began scratching his head as she had many nights before but, at the first touch of her fingers, he cried out:

"Stop! You're burning my ear! There must be some blood on your fingers! Let me see!"

He reached up and caught her hand and, when he saw the blood stains, he flew into a towering rage.

"I thought so! You've been in the forbidden room!"

He jumped up and without allowing her time to say a word he just cut off her head then and there with no more concern than if she had been a mosquito! After that he took the body and the severed head and threw them into the forbidden room and locked the door.

"Now then," he growled, "she won't disobey me again!"

This was all very well but now he had no one to keep house for him and cook and scratch his head in the evening and soon he decided he'd have to get another wife. He remembered that the farmer had two more daughters, so he thought to himself that now he'd marry the second sister.

He waited his chance and one day when the farmer was out in his boat fishing, old Wetehinen came up from the bottom of the lake and clutched the boat. When the poor old farmer tried to row back to shore he couldn't make the boat move an inch. He worked and worked at the oars and wicked old Wetehinen let him struggle until he was exhausted. Then he put his head up out of the water and over the side of the boat and as though nothing were the matter he said:

"Hullo!"

"Oh!" the farmer cried, wishing he were safe on shore, "it's you, is it? I wondered what was holding my boat."

"Yes," wicked old Wetehinen said, "it's me and I'm going to hold your boat right here on this spot until you promise to give me another of your daughters."

What could the farmer do? He pleaded with Wetehinen but Wetehinen was firm and the upshot was that before the farmer again walked dry land he had promised Wetehinen his second daughter.

Well, when he got home, he pretended he had forgotten his ax in the boat and sent his second daughter down to the lake to get it. Wicked old Wetehinen caught her as he had caught her sister and carried her home with him to his house at the bottom of the lake.

Wetehinen treated the second sister just exactly as he had the first, making her mistress of the house and telling her she might use every key but one. Like her sister she, too, after a time gave way to the temptation of looking into the forbidden room and when she saw the shining ring lying in the pool of blood of course she wanted it and of course when she reached to get it she dabbled her fingers in the blood. So that was the end of her, too, for wicked old Wetehinen when he saw the blood stains just cut her head right off and threw her body and the severed head into the forbidden room beside the body and head of her sister and locked the door.

Time went by and the farmer was living happily with his youngest daughter when one day while he was out chopping wood he found a pair of fine birch bark brogues. He put them on and instantly found himself walking away from the woods and down to the lake. He tried to stop but he couldn't. He tried to walk in another direction but the brogues carried him straight down to the water's edge and out into the lake until he was in waist deep.

Then he heard a gruff voice saying:

"Hullo, there! What are you doing with my brogues?"

Of course it was wicked old Wetehinen who had played that trick to get the farmer into his power again.

"What do you want this time?" the poor farmer cried.

"I want your youngest daughter," Wetehinen said.

"What! My youngest daughter!"

"Yes."

"I won't give her up!" the farmer declared. "I don't care what you do to me. I won't give her up!"

"Oh, very well!" Wetehinen said, and immediately the brogues which had been standing still while they talked started walking again. They carried the farmer out into the lake farther and farther until the water was up to his chin.

"Wait—wait a minute!" he cried.

The brogues stopped walking and Wetehinen said:

"Well, do you promise to give her to me?"

"No!" the farmer began. "She's my last daughter and—"

Before he could say more, the brogues walked on and the water rose to his nose. In desperation he threw up his hands and shouted:

"I promise! I promise!"

So when he got home that day he said to his youngest daughter whose name was Lisa:

"Lisa, my dear, I forgot my brogues at the lake. Like a good girl won't you run and get them for me?"

So Lisa went to the lake and Wetehinen of course caught her and carried her down to his house as he had her two sisters.

Then the same old story was repeated. Wetehinen made Lisa mistress of the house and gave her keys to all the doors and closets with the same prohibition against opening the door of the forbidden room.

"If I am mistress of the house," Lisa said to herself, "why should I not unlock every door?"

She waited until one day when Wetehinen was away from home, then went boldly to the forbidden room, fitted the key in the lock, and flung open the door.

There lay her two poor sisters with their heads cut off. There in the pool of blood sparkled the lovely ring, but Lisa paid no heed to it.

"Wicked old Wetehinen!" Lisa cried. "I suppose he thinks that ring will tempt me but nothing will tempt me to touch that awful blood!"

Then she rummaged about, opening boxes and chests, and turning things over. In a dark corner she found two pitchers, one marked Water of Life, the other Water of Death.

"Ha! This is what I want!" she cried, taking the pitcher of the Water of Life.

She set the severed heads of her sisters in place and then with the magic water brought them back to life. She used up all the Water of Life, so she filled the pitcher marked Water of Life with the water from the other pitcher, the Water of Death. She hid her sisters each in a big wooden chest, she shut and locked the door of the forbidden room, and Wetehinen when he came home found her working at her spinning wheel as though nothing unusual had happened.

After supper Wetehinen said:

"Now scratch my head and make me drowsy for bed."

So Lisa scratched his wicked old head and she did it so well that he grunted with satisfaction.

"Uh! Uh!" he said. "That's good! Now just behind my right ear! That's it! That's it! You're a good girl, you are! You're not like some of them who do what they're told not to do! Now behind the other ear! Oh, that's fine! Yes, you're a good girl and if there's anything you want me to do just tell me what it is."

"I want to send a chest of things to my poor old father," Lisa said. "Just a lot of little nothings—odds and ends that I've picked up about the house. I'd be ashamed to have you open the chest and see them. I do wish you'd carry the chest ashore to-morrow and leave it where my father will find it."

"All right, I will," Wetehinen promised.

He was true to his word. The next morning he hoisted one of the chests on his shoulder, the one that had in it the eldest sister, he trudged off with it, and tossed it up on shore at a place where he was sure the farmer would find it.

Lisa then wheedled him into carrying up the second chest that had in it the second sister. This time Wetehinen wasn't so good-natured.

"I don't know what she can always be sending her father!" he grumbled. "If she sends another chest I'll have to look inside and see."

Now Lisa, when the second sister was safely delivered, began to plan her own escape. She pulled out another empty chest and then one evening after she had succeeded in making old Wetehinen comfortable and drowsy she begged him to carry this also to her father. He grumbled and protested but finally promised.

"And you won't look inside, will you? Promise me you won't!" Lisa begged.

Wetehinen said he wouldn't, but he intended to just the same.

Well, the next morning as soon as Wetehinen went out, Lisa took the churn and dressed it up in some of her own clothes. She carried it to the top of the house and perched it on the ridge of the roof before a spinning wheel. Then she herself crept inside the third chest and waited.

When Wetehinen came home he looked up and saw what he thought was Lisa spinning on the roof.

"Hullo!" he shouted. "What are you doing up there?"

Lisa, in the chest, answered in a voice that sounded as if it came from the roof:

"I'm spinning. And you, Wetehinen, my dear, don't forget the chest that you promised to carry to my poor old father. It's standing in the kitchen."

Wetehinen grumbled but because of his promise he hoisted the chest on his shoulder and started off. When he had gone a little way he thought to put it down and take a peep inside. Instantly Lisa's voice, sounding as if it came from the roof, cried out:

"No! No! You promised not to look inside!"

"I'm not looking inside!" Wetehinen called back. "I'm only resting a minute!"

Then he thought to himself:

"I suppose she's sitting up there so she can watch me!"

When he had gone some distance farther, he thought again to set down the chest and open the lid but instantly Lisa's voice, as from a long way off, called out:

"No! No! You promised not to look inside!"

"Who's looking inside?" he called back, pretending again he was only resting.

Every time he thought it would be safe to put down the chest and open the lid, Lisa's voice cried out:

"No! No! You promised not to!"

"Mercy on us!" old Wetehinen fumed to himself, "who would have thought she could see so far!"

On the shore of the lake when he threw down the chest in disgust he tried one last time to raise the lid. Instantly Lisa's voice cried out:

"No! No! You promised not to!"

"I'm not looking inside!" Wetehinen roared, and in a fury he left the chest and started back into the water.

All the way home he grumbled and growled:

"A nice way to treat a man, always making him carry chests! I won't carry another one no matter how much she begs me!"

When he came near home he saw the spinning wheel still on the roof and the figure still seated before it.

"Why haven't you got my dinner ready?" he called out angrily.

The figure at the spinning wheel made no answer.

"What's the matter with you?" Wetehinen cried. "Why are you sitting there like a wooden image instead of cooking my dinner?"

Still the figure made no answer and in a rage Wetehinen began climbing up the roof. He reached out blindly and clutched at Lisa's skirt and jerked it so hard that the churn came clattering down on his head. It knocked him off the roof and he fell all the way to the ground and cracked his wicked old head wide open.

"Ouch! Ouch!" he roared in pain. "Just wait till I get hold of that Lisa!"

He crawled to the forbidden room and poured over himself the water that was in the pitcher marked Water of Life. But it wasn't the Water of Life at all, it was the Water of Death, and so it didn't help his wicked old cracked head at all. In fact it just made it worse and worse and worse.

Lisa and her sisters were never again troubled by him nor was any one else that lived on the shores of that lake.

"Wonder what's become of wicked old Wetehinen?" people began saying.

Lisa thought she knew but she didn't tell.

THE ORIGIN
of the NARRAN LAKE

Australia

Old Byamee said to his two young wives, Birrahgnooloo and Cunnunbeillee, "I have stuck a white feather between the hind legs of a bee, and am going to let it go and then follow it to its nest, that I may get honey. While I go for the honey, go you two out and get frogs and yams, then meet me at Coorigel Spring, where we will camp, for sweet and clear is the water there."

The wives, taking their goolays and yam sticks, went out as he told them. Having gone far, and dug out many yams and frogs, they were tired when they reached Coorigel, and, seeing the cool, fresh water, they longed to bathe. But first they built a bough shade, and there left their goolays holding their food, and the yams and frogs they had found. When their camp was ready for the coming of Byamee, who having wooed his wives with a nullah-nullah, kept them obedient by fear of the same weapon, then went the girls to the spring to bathe. Gladly they plunged in, having first divested themselves of their goomillahs, which they were still young enough to wear, and which they left on the ground near the spring. Scarcely were they enjoying the cool rest the water gave their hot, tired limbs, when they were seized and swallowed by two kurreahs.

Having swallowed the girls, the kurreahs dived into an opening in the side of the spring, which was the entrance to an underground watercourse leading to the Narran River. Through this passage they went, taking all the water from the spring with them into the Narran, whose course they also dried as they went along.

Meantime Byamee, unwitting the fate of his wives, was honey hunting. He had followed the bee with the white feather on it for some distance; then the bee flew on to some budtha flowers, and would move no further. Byamee said, "Something has happened, or the bee would not stay here and refuse to be moved on towards its nest. I must go to Coorigel Spring and see if my wives are safe. Something terrible has surely happened." And Byamee turned in haste towards the spring.

When he reached there he saw the bough shed his wives had made, he saw the yams they had dug from the ground, and he saw the frogs, but Birrahgnooloo and Cunnunbeillee he saw not. He called aloud for them. But no answer. He went towards the spring; on the edge of it he saw the goomillahs of his wives. He looked into the spring and, seeing it dry, he said, "It is the work of the kurreahs; they have opened the underground passage and gone with my wives to the river, and opening the passage has dried the spring. Well do I know where the passage joins the Narran, and there will I swiftly go."

Arming himself with spears and woggarahs he started in pursuit. He soon reached the deep hole where the underground channel of the Coorigel joined the Narran. There he saw what he had never seen before, namely, this deep hole dry. And he said: "They have emptied the holes as they went along, taking the water with them. But well know I the deep holes of the river. I will not follow the bend, thus trebling the distance I have to go, but I will cut across from big hole to big hole, and by so doing I may yet get ahead of the kurreahs."

On swiftly sped Byamee, making short cuts from big hole to big hole, and his track is still marked by the morilla ridges that stretch down the Narran, pointing in towards the deep holes. Every hole as he came to it he found dry, until at last he reached the end of the Narran; the hole there was still quite wet and muddy, then he knew he was near his enemies, and soon he saw them.

He managed to get, unseen, a little way ahead of the kurreahs. He hid himself behind a big dheal tree. As the kurreahs came near they separated, one turning to go in another direction. Quickly Byamee hurled one spear after another, wounding both kurreahs, who writhed with pain and lashed their tails furiously, making great hollows in the ground, which the water they had brought with them quickly filled. Thinking they might again escape him, Byamee drove them from the water with his spears, and then, at close quarters, he killed them with his woggarahs. And ever afterwards at flood time, the Narran flowed into this hollow which the kurreahs in their writhings had made.

When Byamee saw that the kurreahs were quite dead, he cut them open and took out the bodies of his wives. They were covered with wet slime, and seemed quite lifeless; but he carried them and laid them on two nests of red ants. Then he sat down at some little distance and watched them. The ants quickly covered the bodies, cleaned them rapidly of the wet slime, and soon Byamee noticed the muscles of the girls twitching. "Ah," he said, "there is life, they feel the sting of the ants."

Almost as he spoke came a sound as of a thunder-clap, but the sound seemed to come from the ears of the girls. And as the echo was dying away, slowly the girls rose to their feet. For a moment they stood apart, a dazed expression on their faces. Then they clung together, shaking as if stricken with a deadly fear. But Byamee came to them and explained how they had been rescued from the kurreahs by him. He bade them to beware of ever bathing in the deep holes of the Narran, lest such holes be the haunt of kurreahs.

Then he bade them look at the water now at Boogira, and he said:

"Soon will the black swans find their way here, the pelicans and the ducks; where there was dry land and stones in the past, in the future there will be water and water-fowl, from henceforth; when the Narran runs it will run into this hole, and by the spreading of its waters will a big lake be made." And what Byamee said has come to pass, as the Narran Lake shows, with its large sheet of water, spreading for miles, the home of thousands of wild fowl.

NOT AS
THEY SEEM

THE PRINCESS
and the GHOULS

India

Once upon a time a certain king went out hunting in the forest. After chasing his game the whole day, he found a wild, fierce woman sitting alone, who, as soon as he came near, sprang to her feet and caught hold of his reins.

"Who are you?" cried the startled king. "Are you a woman or a demon? Let my horse go!"

"My name is What-will-be-will-be," replied the woman, "and one day I shall make you feel my power."

The king asked her: "But when will this thing be?"

"Choose, O king," answered she," whether I shall bring it upon you now or at some distant period!"

"Let me not answer you now," said the king; "let me first go and consult my queen, and I will return and tell you."

"Go," said the fierce old hag; "I shall await you here."

So the king rode home, and as he entered his palace his looks were distressed. Said the queen to him: "Your looks betoken trouble; what is the matter?"

"Oh, do not ask me what is the matter!" answered he. "I met in the forest an old witch named What-will-be-will-be, and she has bidden me choose whether adversity shall fall upon us now or hereafter. What shall I tell her?"

"You and I," replied the queen, "are both of us young and strong. Choose, then, that the trouble may visit us soon, while we are well able to meet and to bear it."

Then the king returned to the forest, and to the old woman, whom he found in the same spot, he said: "Whatever is to befall us, let it come now, and not hereafter."

"Be it so," answered the woman. "You have your wish."

Scarcely had the king arrived at his capital when a mounted messenger met him and informed him that the king of another country was at hand with a vast army to make war upon him. In the battle which ensued this unfortunate monarch was totally routed, and his kingdom fell into the hands of his enemy. But he himself, with his queen and the two princes his sons, and his sons' two wives, having all armed themselves, and having mounted upon swift horses, fled away from the city and escaped.

On and on they went, as strangers in strange lands, until at last the whole of their money was expended, and poverty and want began to stare them in the face. Then the king said to himself: "If we could only leave my sons' wives somewhere, and steal away from them unperceived, our troubles would diminish, for we should have fewer mouths to provide for."

Having formed this cruel design, he soon carried it into practice, and one night, when the two young princesses were wrapt in slumber, the rest of the party, leaving the unfortunate girls a couple of horses and some arms, abandoned them in the wilderness.

When the two princesses awoke, they looked about them, and found themselves alone; and having cried for their friends in vain, they began to say to each other, "What shall we do now?"

"If we both travel in these wild places as women," said the elder and wiser sister, "we shall be robbed and cruelly treated."

So she set to work, and in a short time she had altered her feminine robes into a man's attire, and having assumed her arms, she mounted her horse, and she then looked a noble young prince, both valiant and strong, while her beautiful sister, in her own raiment, rode beside her. The two princesses now set out again to search for their friends, but they rode and searched in vain. No signs of them were to be discovered or seen, neither could they hear any tidings of them.

One day they came to a certain city where there was a king, and in this city the elder sister determined to tarry. So she took a small house for herself and her sister, and every day in her masculine disguise, mounted, and armed with sword and lance, she attended the court of the king, until at last the king observed her, and said to his vizier: "Who is that stranger who comes every day to court?"

Then the minister approached the princess, and asked her: "Who are you? Are you a king's son or a merchant's son? What are you, and whence came you?"

"I am in need of nothing," answered the princess. "I am merely looking for a lost brother."

Then the king called for her, and said to her: "If honourable service were offered to you, would you accept it?"

"Yes," answered the girl, but only to become one of your own body-guard."

The king, who had taken a fancy to this handsome youth, as he supposed the princess to be, immediately made out an order for her, and she was enrolled as a member of his body-guard.

Her duties were light and her payment liberal. She was most assiduous to please, watching the king with careful fidelity whenever she was on guard; ever active and alert, but never forgetting that her chief concern was to scan the faces of all new-comers, if by any chance her own friends should be among them.

Now, it was a custom in that country that if a criminal were sentenced to death he should be conducted by the executioners to a wild place and hanged on a tree or a gallows, and there at once abandoned, either to escape if he could, or to be the prey of the vultures.

One evening, when the princess was on sentry over the king, a notorious robber was thus taken out and hanged. In the middle of the night the princess heard a dismal howling and wailing, and fearing that some danger was approaching, she boldly entered the forest to find out the cause of the disturbance. In a few minutes she came to the gallows-tree, on which the dead robber was swaying in the wind, and under the tree she noticed what appeared to be a miserable gaunt woman, who from time to time set up the dismal howling which had so greatly alarmed her. In reality, however, the creature was not a woman, but a female ghoul—that is, a demon in human form, who, like the vampire, wanders about at night and feeds upon corpses.

"Who are you?" demanded the princess.

"This man who has been hanged is my son," answered the monster. "He hangs too high for me to reach him, for I am old and feeble. If you would lift me up, O strong young sir, I might perhaps kiss him once more, as I shall never see his face again."

The princess, who did not suspect her true character, raised her up to the body; but the ghoul, instead of kissing it, seized it by the neck with her teeth, and began to suck the blood. Perceiving this horror, the princess instantly dropped her, and, drawing her sword, she struck at her; but the ghoul evaded the stroke and fled. Nevertheless, the princess had severed a piece of her clothing, which she picked up, and, examining it, she found it was composed of the very richest material, worked in strange and fantastic figures, with threads of gold.

Returning at once to the palace, the princess found the king sitting up awake. "You are posted here," said he, "to guard me from intrusion. Where have you been?"

Then the princess related to the king the whole story, telling him of the dismal wailings and of the female ghoul who had sucked the blood of the robber. The king was incredulous, and said to her: "Have you any proof of the truth of this extraordinary adventure?"

Then she showed him the piece of cloth, which the king inspected with astonishment and admiration. "This cloth," said he, "is of the rarest quality and most precious."

He was so pleased that he gave the princess a bag of gold, and sent the cloth as a present to the queen his wife, who, as soon as she had seen and examined it, longed for more of it, and so she sent word to the king: "Such beautiful cloth has never before been seen in the kingdom. I would have a whole suit of it."

The king now said to the princess: "Wherever it was you obtained this wonderful cloth, you must depart instantly and fetch me more of the same pattern."

The princess was amazed at such an order, and answered: "Who knows whence the ghoul came or whither she has gone? Where am I to look for her?"

This objection the king merely waved aside. "If you bring the cloth it will be well with you," said he, "but if not, your head shall answer for it!"

"Be it so," said the princess, with confidence. "But, O king, grant me time."

To this request the king assented, and, giving her both time and abundance of money, ordered her to set out forthwith.

The next morning she bade her sister farewell, and started on her quest of the ghoul's coat. Many a day she journeyed, until at last she found herself in the territories of another king. In the midst of this kingdom she arrived at a half-abandoned city, where grass was growing in the streets, and where the few inhabitants wore a melancholy and woe-begone aspect. Here she perceived an old woman surrounded by one or two others, all of whom were kneading huge quantities of dough. As she gazed in wonder, she noticed that the old woman was crying and lamenting.

"O mother," said the princess, "you are both baking bread and crying! What is the matter?"

"Every eighth day a ghoul comes here," answered she—"a monster from the mountains; and the tribute he receives by the king's order is a human being, a buck goat, and two hundred pounds of bread. The reason I am crying is that to-day it is my turn, and that I have to give the ghoul my only son."

Then said the princess to the old woman, "Mother, do not cry. When you have the bread ready, let it be taken with the goat to the usual place, and thither I also will go instead of your son."

"But who in the world," said the woman, "would give his life for another?"

Now, the king of that country had made an order that whosoever should kill or drive away the ghoul should be rewarded with riches and honoured with the hand of one of his daughters. And the princess, having heard of this order, turned to the old woman, and said: "But is no one able to kill the ghoul?"

"No one whatever," answered she.

"Well," said the princess, "at least come and show me the place where he is accustomed to feed."

When the bread was all ready, the old woman and her son, and the buck goat, proceeded with the princess to the spot. In that dismal place, which lay without the city-walls, there stood an old hut, and there the whole tribute used to be put for the ghoul, who always came at night and devoured it all before the morning.

Going into the hut, the princess first dug a great hole. Then she placed the goat and the heap of bread on one side, and on the other she set up a log of wood dressed up to look in the darkness like a boy. Having completed these arrangements, she dismissed the old woman and her friends, and descended herself into the pit, where, with her sword ready drawn in her hand, she crouched down and hid herself. In the middle of the night she heard a roar, and the ghoul, in the form of a gigantic man, rushed into the hut and began to devour. When he had eaten the bread and the buck goat, he went to the log and seized it ravenously. At that moment the princess rose from her pit, and smote and cut off one of his legs, which so startled the brute that he instantly fled from the hut on his other leg, and made his escape to the hills with the utmost despatch.

In the morning the princess returned to the city, and said to the old woman: "I had an encounter with the ghoul last night, and he has been punished so handsomely that he will never trouble you or your neighbours again."

Everyone was astonished, and some cried "Nonsense!" but the most hopeless were convinced when the princess displayed to them the monster's horrid leg. Then the old woman gave away both money and food in charity for the sake of their glorious deliverer, and because of herself and her son, whom he had delivered from destruction.

When the king, who dwelt in the citadel, heard the news of this exploit he also was surprised beyond measure, and he sent for the princess and treated her with the utmost honour.

"How did you manage to accomplish this great achievement?" asked he.

Then the princess told him the history of her adventure without adding to or diminishing aught from the simple truth.

The king listened with gratified interest, and rewarded the heroine by saying to her: "It is a decree of mine that whoso shall kill the ghoul or drive him out of my dominions shall receive the hand of my daughter in marriage. The lady is ready, and, therefore, if you are willing to marry her, pray do so."

The princess was more than grateful for this proof of the king's generosity and goodwill, yet she answered him: "O king, I have still another enterprise on hand, but when that is safely accomplished I shall again return to your court."

The king then suffered her to depart, and so, mounting her horse, she travelled on and on again for weeks and months. At last, in the midst of craggy mountains and gloomy defiles belonging to a third kingdom, she came to a lonely fortress with frowning walls and forbidding appearance. Entering the open gateway, she found herself in a courtyard, and there she saw a gentle maiden sitting spinning, but no one else was visible anywhere. When the girl saw the princess, she first laughed, and then she cried. The princess was amazed, and, going up to her, she said: "Why do you both laugh and cry?"

"Never since the day of my birth" answered the girl, "have I seen a man; and when I saw you, therefore, I laughed. But I cried because the ghouls who live in this castle will certainly eat you up."

"How many ghouls are there?" asked the princess.

"There are two of them," answered the girl, "and one of them is the husband of the other."

"But is there no way of escape for me?" inquired the princess.

"For this one night," said the girl, "I may be able to save you from them, but not for more."

She then rose, and with looks of love conducted the princess to a lonely chamber, and having left some food and some water with her, she fastened the door and came away.

As the shadows began to fall, the two ghouls returned to their gloomy castle, bringing with them some buck goats and the remains of a human being. Having made their horrid evening meal, they poured out quantities of wine into golden goblets and began to quaff and to make merry. Then, looking at the girl, one of them said to the other: "About this girl of ours, whom we stole as a baby: it is time that we should find a husband for her. If now we could capture a brave man, we might marry them together."

"I could recognise the man who cut off the skirt of my coat," answered the female ghoul. "If we could find him, we might marry her to him, for a braver man never lived."

" Ah," replied the male ghoul, "but he was a braver man a great deal who cut off my leg."

The two ghouls now began to dispute and to fall out as to which of the two men was the braver, the male ghoul asserting that the girl should be married to the man who cut off his leg, and the female protesting that she should be the wife of the man who cut off the end of her embroidered coat. And so they fell asleep.

In the morning the two ghouls went away as usual to hunt for man's flesh, and the girl, going to the secret chamber, released the princess from her lonely tower, and brought her forth, telling her as she did so all that had passed between the two ghouls the night before.

"But," continued she, "I would rather marry you, dear prince, if the ghouls would allow me."

Then the princess inquired further into their history, and the girl told her the story of the ghouls' misfortunes: how one lost part of her garment, and the other his leg.

" But," said the princess, "it was I who deprived them of both; I cut off the leg of the one, and I cut off some of the cloak of the other. Would they, then, give you to me?"

"They would be most willing to do so," replied the girl, astonished and pleased.

That day passed in visiting the rooms of the castle and in wondering at its vast treasures and stores of all manner of rarities, and in the evening the princess was again hidden in the secret chamber.

When the ghouls returned, they feasted and caroused as before, and when warmed with wine they again began to dispute as to who should marry the girl, each, without knowing it, extolling the bravery of the same hero. Then said the girl: "But perhaps it was the one man who achieved both those wonderful exploits. If so, would you allow him to marry me?"

" Marry you?" cried they. "Of course he should marry you, and take you wherever he pleased."

"Then," said the girl, "give me your most solemn assurance that, if he can be found, you will not kill him."

"We make the promise, of course," said they.

Then, going to the secret chamber, the girl brought forth the princess, and took her in before them, and both the savages, at once recognising her, gazed at her with wonder, admiration, and astonishment.

"How did you contrive so well to cut off my leg?" asked the male ghoul.

"I dug a hole in the floor of the hut," answered the undaunted princess, "and in that I hid myself, and the goat and the bread I put on one side, and a dressed-up log on the other; and when you passed by me to seize the log, I raised my sword and at a blow off came your leg."

"Wonderful!" cried the male ghoul, in tones of awe.

"And how did you cut off the skirt of my coat?" asked the female ghoul.

"When I saw what a monster you were," answered the princess, "and when I heard you sucking the blood of the dead robber, I dropped you on the ground, and, drawing my sword, I made a stroke at you, and thus it was that I cut off the skirt of your coat."

"O most wonderful prince!" cried the female ghoul, equally amazed.

Then said they: "Now take away this girl with you. You have won her; she is yours. Take her to your own country, and marry her."

When the princess and her bride were all ready for the journey, the ghouls loaded them with heaps of money and presents.

"One thing only I care for," said the princess, "and that is the coat of embroidered gold of which I have already a piece."

Her wish was no sooner expressed than it was gratified; and for the sake of the girl the ghouls presented her with much more of the same material as well. After this they accompanied the pair to the borders of their own territory, and there they left them.

Journeying on, the princess and her young bride arrived at the city which had formerly suffered so greatly from the exactions of the male ghoul. The king was enchanted to welcome her back, and gave her his daughter in marriage in accordance with his promise, together with riches in abundance; after which she continued her journey to the country of her own king; and having arrived at the capital, she committed her two wives to the custody of her younger sister, and at once rode on to the palace. There she presented the whole of the wonderful cloth which she had brought from the castle of the ghouls; and the king was so delighted that he instantly said to her: "Now you shall be my prime minister, and you shall live in a palace of your own."

"Very well," answered the princess, and at once the order was made out, the decree published, and she was promoted to the head of affairs.

The princess was now both powerful and wealthy, but she never for a moment forgot the one object of her life, which was to find her lost friends. With this thought ever present in her mind, she one day said to the king: "If you will allow me, I would make a large garden to contain trees and plants of every kind."

The king approved of her plan, and gave her an immense tract of land for the purpose. Her design was that her garden should be the wonder of the whole world, and so there was not a country to which she did not send her messengers to make known that whosoever would bring her a plant for her garden should receive two gold mohurs. But all the time she was thinking of her dear friends, and hoping that in their poverty and obscurity, wherever they were, they might hear tidings of her wonderful garden, and be induced to bring her some plants for the sake of the reward.

For months this good princess was doomed to disappointment, for, though thousands came with plants of the rarest varieties, her own relations came not. At last the king, her first father-in-law, in his distant exile, heard the proclamation, and, as he was very poor, he and the queen his wife, and their two sons, searched for the rarest plants, and carried them to the famous garden. There, notwithstanding their altered condition, their ragged clothing, and their attenuated frames, they were immediately recognised by the princess. But she refrained herself, and ordered them to be confined in a certain house, over which she placed a guard, while at the same time she herself occupied a room in which she could overhear all they spoke about.

The first thing the king said was: "Strange! all others receive rewards and are allowed to depart, but we only are placed here under restraint."

"I suppose," said the queen, "we are being punished by God for having so cruelly abandoned those two poor girls in the desert."

No longer able to restrain herself, the princess left the house and at once ordered her friends to be conducted into sumptuous chambers, and to be supplied with baths and rich clothing, and with food and wine of the best. Then she had them all brought into her own palace, and, in her character and disguise of prime minister of the kingdom, she received them as if for the purpose of a mere audience, nor had any of them any suspicion of her real identity. Having seated them on chairs, she gazed on them, and said: "What is your history?"

"We were once a royal family," answered the aged king, "but misfortune befell us, and we were driven from our kingdom. Then, in our need and distress, we abandoned the young wives of my two sons in a lonely place, and ever since we have lived poor, unblest and unknown."

"Yes," said the princess, "I suppose you left the princesses because of your necessity. Notwithstanding, every child of man has to eat his own kismet."

Then she left the room, and for the first time for years she assumed her own proper habit; and taking her sister by the hand, she led her into the apartment, and looking at the young princes, their husbands, she said: "You left behind in the desert your two wives, but now God has restored them to you once more."

Then she turned to the king and queen, and there followed many a fond embrace, with tears and words of surprise and of love, and they were all reunited in a lasting reconciliation.

The next morning the princess went to the king, and said to him: "The time has come when I must reveal to you the secret of my life. No longer a man, I now assume my proper character, for I am really the wife of a prince of ancient lineage, and my husband is here."

Then she related the story of her life, and said: "And now assist us with a suitable army, that we may take the field and recover our own lost inheritance. But if not, then permit me to remain here, and give my friends positions near your own person."

"Choose," said the king, "which you will have."

"Let us, then, have the troops," answered she, "and the treasure to wage a campaign."

To this proposal the king joyfully agreed, and the princess, with all her friends, set out at the head of an invincible army, and having routed the usurper in a signal battle, they recovered their lost dominion, and the old king ascended his throne and reigned once more. Then, having provided splendid matches for the two beautiful girls whom the princess had married in her expedition against the ghouls, the whole united family settled down in peace and prosperity, and lived happily ever afterwards.

My story is about earthly Kings, but the true King is God.[1]

---

1.   Panjabis generally begin and sometimes end their stories of kings with this confession of faith.

THE BUSO-MONKEY

❦

Philippines (Bagobo)

One day a man went out, carrying seventeen arrows, to hunt monkeys; but he found none. Next day he went again, and, as he walked along on the slope of the mountain called Malagū'san, he heard the sound of the chattering of monkeys in the trees. Looking up, he saw the great monkey sitting on an alumā'yag-tree. He took a shot at the monkey, but his arrow missed aim; and the next time he had no better luck. Twice eight he tried it; but he never hit the mark. The monkey seemed to lead a charmed life. Finally he took his seventeenth and last arrow, and brought down his game; the monkey fell down dead. But a voice came from the monkey's body that said, "You must carry me."

So the man picked up the monkey, and started to go back home; but on the way the monkey said, "You are to make a fire, and eat me up right here."

Then the man laid the monkey on the ground. Again came the voice, "You will find a bamboo to put me in; by and by you shall eat me."

Off went the man to find the bamboo called laya, letting the monkey lie on the ground, where he had dropped it.

He walked on until he reached a forest of bamboo. There, swinging on a branch of the laya, was a karirik-bird. And the bird chirped to the man, "Where are you going?"

The man answered, "I am looking for bamboo to put the monkey in."

But the karirik-bird exclaimed, "Run away, quick! for by and by the monkey will become a buso. I will wait here, and be cutting the laya; then, when the monkey calls you, I will answer him."

In the mean time the monkey had become a great buso. He had only one eye, and that stood right in the middle of his forehead, looking just like the big bowl called langungan (the very bad buso have only one eye; some have only one leg).

After the Buso-monkey had waited many hours for the man to come back, he started out to look for him. When he reached the forest of laya, he called to the man, "Where are you?"

Then the karirik-bird answered from the tree, "Here I am, right here, cutting the bamboo."

But the man had run away, because the bird had sent him off, and made him run very fast.

As soon as the bird had answered the Buso, it flew off to another bamboo-tree, and there the Buso spied it, and knew that he had been fooled; and he said, "It's a man I want; you're just a bird. I don't care for you."

Directly then the Buso began to smell around the ground where the man had started to run up the mountain-side, and, as quick as he caught the scent, he trailed the man. He ran and ran, and all the time the man was running too; but soon the Buso began to gain on him. After a while, when the Buso had come close upon him, the man tried to look for some covert. He reached a big rock, and cried out, "O rock! will you give me shelter when the Buso tries to eat me?"

"No," replied the rock; "for, if I should help you, the Buso would break me off and throw me away."

Then the man ran on; and the Buso came nearer and nearer, searching behind every rock as he rushed along, and spying up into every tree, to see if, perchance, the man were concealed there.

At last the man came to the lemon-tree called kabayawa, that has long, sharp thorns on its branches. And the man cried out to the lemon-tree, "Could you protect me, if I were to hide among your leaves and flowers?"

Instantly the lemon-tree answered, "Come right up, if you want to."

Then the man climbed the tree, and concealed himself in the branches, among the flowers. Very soon the Buso came under the lemon-tree, and shouted to it, "I smell a man here. You are hiding him."

The Kabayawa said, "Sure enough, here's a man! You just climb up and get him."

Then the Buso began to scramble up the tree; but as he climbed, the thorns stuck their sharp points into him. The higher he climbed, the longer and sharper grew the thorns of the tree, piercing and tearing, until they killed the Buso.

It is because the monkey sometimes turns into a Buso that many Bagobo refuse to eat monkey. But some of the mountain Bagobo eat monkey to keep off sores.

THE BIRD of SORROW

Turkey

In very remote times there lived a Padishah whose daughter was so much attached to her governess that she scarcely ever left her side. One day, seeing the latter deep in thought, the Princess asked: "Of what are you thinking?" "I have sorrow," answered the governess. "What is sorrow?" questioned the Padishah's daughter; "let me also have it." "It is well," said the woman, and went to the tscharschi, where she bought a Bird of Sorrow in a cage. She presented it to the maiden, who was so delighted that she amused herself day and night with the creature.

Some time afterwards the Sultan's daughter, attended by her slaves, paid a visit to the Zoo. She took with her the bird in its cage, which she hung upon the branch of a tree. Suddenly the bird commenced to speak. "Set me free a little while, Sultana," it pleaded, "that I may play with the other birds. I will come back again." The Princess accordingly set her favourite at liberty.

A few hours later, while the Princess was sauntering idly about the park, the bird returned, seized its mistress, and flew off with her to the top of a high mountain. "Behold! this is sorrow," said the bird; "I will prepare more of it for you!" Saying this he flew away.

The Princess, now hungry and thirsty, wandered about until she met a herdsman, with whom she exchanged raiment, so that she might disguise herself as a man for her better protection. After long wandering she came to a village where, finding a coffeehouse, she entered, and besought the proprietor to engage her as his assistant. The former, regarding her as a young man in need of employment, accordingly engaged her, and towards evening went home, leaving her in charge of the house.

Having closed the shop, the girl lay down to sleep. At midnight, however, the Bird of Sorrow appeared, broke all the cups and saucers and nargiles in the place, woke the maiden from her sleep, and thus addressed her: "Behold! this is sorrow; I will prepare more of it for you!" Having thus spoken he flew away as before. All night long the poor girl lay thinking what she should say to her master on the morrow. When morning came the proprietor returned, and seeing the woeful damage done, beat his assistant severely and drove her away.

Her eyes filled with bitter tears, she set out once more, and ere many hours arrived at a tailor's shop. As preparations were being made for the great religious feast of Bairam, the tailor was busy in executing orders for the serai. He was therefore in need of an extra hand, and took the youth, as he supposed the girl to be, into his service. After a day or two the tailor went away, leaving the maiden alone in the house. When evening came she closed the shop and retired to rest. At midnight came the bird again, and tore to shreds all the clothes on the premises, and waking up the girl, said: "Behold! this is sorrow; I will prepare still more of it for you!" and flew off again. Next morning brought the master, who seeing the clothing all torn up, called his assistant to account. As the girl answered nothing, the master beat her soundly and sent her away.

Weeping bitterly she once more set forth, and by and by came to a fringe-maker's, where she was taken in. Being again left alone, she fell asleep. The Bird of Sorrow reappeared, tore up the fringes, woke the girl, made his customary speech, and flew away as on previous occasions.

When the master returned next morning and saw the mischief, he beat his assistant more cruelly than ever, and dismissed her. Overwhelmed with grief, the unhappy maiden again took her lonely way. Feeling sure that the Bird of Sorrow would give her no peace, she went into a mountain pass, where she lived in seclusion for many days, suffering the pangs of hunger and thirst, and in constant fear of the wild beasts that haunted the region. Her nights were spent in the leafy branches of a tree.

One day the son of a Padishah, when out hunting, espied the girl in the tree. Mistaking her for a bird, he shot an arrow at her, but it merely struck one of the branches. On approaching the tree to reclaim his arrow, the Shahzada observed that what he had supposed to be a bird appeared to be a man. "Are you an in or a jin?" he called out. "Neither in nor jin," was the response, "but a human creature like yourself." Whereupon the Prince permitted her to descend from the tree, and took the seeming herdsman to the palace. Here, after bathing, she resumed the garments of a maiden. Then the royal youth saw that she was beautiful as the moon at the full, and straightway fell violently in love with her. Without delay he besought his father, the Padishah, to consent to his wedding with her. The Sultan commanded the maiden to be brought into his presence, and as he gazed upon her wonderful beauty, her loveliness and grace won his heart. The betrothal took place forthwith; and after a period of festivity lasting forty days and forty nights the marriage was celebrated. In due time a little daughter was born to the princely pair, a child gentle and fair to look upon, and giving early promise of becoming as lovely as its mother.

One midnight came the bird, stole the babe, and besmeared the mother's lips with blood. Then it woke the Princess, and said: "Behold, I am taking away your child; and still more sorrow will I prepare for you!" So saying the bird flew off. In the morning the Prince missed his little daughter, and observed that his wife's lips were blood-stained. Going quickly to his father, the Padishah, he related the ominous occurrence.

"From the mountain did you bring the woman," said the Padishah; "she is forsooth a daughter of the mountain and eats human flesh; therefore I counsel you to send her away!" But the devoted Prince pleaded for his young wife and prevailed over his father.

Some time later another daughter was born to them, which also the bird stole away under similar circumstances. This time the Padishah commanded that the mother should be put to death, though yielding at length to the earnest entreaties of his son he grudgingly consented to pardon her.

Time passed away, and eventually a son was born. The Prince, fearing that if this child also should disappear his beloved wife would surely be put to death, determined to lie awake at night and keep watch and ward over his loved ones. Tired nature, however, insisted on her toll and the Prince slept.

Meanwhile the bird returned, stole the babe, besmeared the Princess's lips with blood as before, and flew away. When the poor mother awoke and discovered her terrible loss, she wept bitterly; and when the Prince also awoke and found the child missing and his wife's mouth and nose dripping with blood, he hastened to his father with the awful intelligence. The Padishah, in a violent rage, again condemned the woman to death. The executioners were summoned; they bound her hands behind her and led her forth to execution. But so smitten were they with her ravishing beauty, and so stricken with pity for her sore affliction, that they said to her:

"We cannot find it in our hearts to kill you. Go where you will, only return not again to the palace."

The poor ill-fated woman again sought her mountain refuge, brooding over her sad lot; until one day the bird once more appeared, seized her, and carried her off to the garden of a grand palace.

Setting down his burden, the bird shook himself, and lo! he was suddenly transformed into a handsome youth. Taking her by the hand, he led the disconsolate woman upstairs into the palace. Here a wonderful sight met her eyes. Attended by many servants, three beautiful children, all radiant and smiling, approached her. As her astonished gaze fell upon them, her eyes filled with tears of joy and her heart melted with tenderness.

Escorting the now happy and wondering Princess into a stately apartment, richly carpeted and furnished with all the art of the luxurious Orient, the youth thus addressed her: "Sultana, though I afflicted you with much grief and sorrow, robbed you of your precious children, and nearly brought you to an ignominious death, yet have you patiently borne it all and not betrayed me. In reward I have built for you this palace, in which I now restore to you your loved ones. Behold your children! Henceforth, Sultana, I am your slave." The Princess hastened with winged feet to her long-lost children, embraced them, pressed them to her bosom, and covered them with kisses.

How fared it with the Prince?

Sorrowing for his children and for his beloved wife, whom he believed to have been put to death, he grew morose and melancholy, passing the time with his old opium smoker, who beguiled the hours with indifferent stories.

One day, having no more opium, the old man requested the Prince's permission to go to the tscharschi in order to buy more. On his way thither he saw something he had never before beheld: a large and magnificent serail! "It is remarkable," thought the old fellow; "I frequent this street daily, yet have I not seen this palace before. When can it have been built? I must inspect it."

The Sultana, whose palace it was, happened to be at one of the windows and caught sight of her husband's opium smoker. The slave—formerly her Bird of Sorrow—being in attendance, he respectfully suggested: "What say you, lady, to playing a trick on the Prince's old storyteller?" At these words he threw a magic rose at the feet of the grey-beard. The latter picked it up, inhaled its exquisite perfume, and muttered to himself: "If your rose is so beautiful, how must it be with yourself!" So instead of returning home he entered the palace.

The Prince in the meantime grew concerned over the prolonged absence of the old man and sent his steward to look for him. The steward, arriving before the palace, the door of which had been left open intentionally by the slave, went in to look round. A number of female slaves received him and led the way up the stairs. At the top he was handed over to the magician slave, who requested him to remove his outer robe and precede him. The robe was taken off without difficulty, but the steward was astonished to find that in spite of all his efforts he was quite unable to remove his fez. At this the magician ordered him to be cast out "for refusing to take off his fez." The steward was therefore forcibly ejected. But no sooner was he outside than—wonderful to relate—the fez fell from his head of its own accord! On his way home he overtook the old opium smoker. Meanwhile the Shahzada was troubled at the non-return of his steward and dispatched his treasurer after him. The treasurer met both on the road and demanded to know what had befallen them. The old opium smoker answered somewhat enigmatically: "If a rose be thrown from that palace, take care not to smell it, or the consequences be on your own head." And the steward warned him no less mysteriously: "When you enter that palace, be sure to leave your fez at the door!"

The treasurer considered the behaviour of both his companions somewhat peculiar, but taking their warning lightly he entered the palace. Inside he was ordered to don a dressing-gown before proceeding upstairs. Commencing to undress for the purpose, he discovered that his schalwar refused to part company with his person. Consequently he was unceremoniously thrown out of the palace. Hardly, however, was he outside than his schalwar came off by itself!

The Prince becoming unable longer to endure the unaccountable absence of his servants, set out himself to discover, if possible, what had happened to them. On the way he met all three, who counselled him in an excited manner: "If a rose be thrown to you from the palace, be careful not to smell it; when you enter, be sure to leave your fez at the door; and before you arrive there, take off your schalwar and enter without it!"

The Prince was exceedingly puzzled at such extraordinary advice, yet he straight-way went to the serail and disappeared from sight within the portal. Unlike his servants, the Prince was received with every mark of honour and respect, and conducted to a noble hall. Here a lady of remarkable beauty, surrounded by three lovely children, awaited him.

The lady gave to her eldest child a stool, to the second a towel, and to the youngest a tray; into the tray she put a bowl, into the bowl a pear, and beside it a spoon. The eldest set the stool on the floor, the second offered the towel to the Prince, while the youngest sat himself down in the bowl. The Prince then inquired of the children: "How long has it been the custom to eat pears with a spoon?" "Since human beings have eaten human flesh," they answered in chorus. The chord of memory was struck; the past flashed before the mind's eye of the Prince. Here the magician appeared and cried: "Oh Prince, behold thy Sultana! Behold also thy children!" Whereat all—father, mother, and children—fell on each other's necks weeping for joy.

The magician continued: "My Shahzada, I am your slave; if, however, you deign to give me my liberty, I will hasten to my own parents."

Overflowing with gratitude for their reunion, they immediately set the magician slave free and prepared a new festival, happy in the knowledge that hence-forth they would never be parted from each other.

THE UNKTOMI (SPIDER),
TWO WIDOWS,
and the RED PLUMS

Great Sioux Nation

There once lived, in a remote part of a great forest, two widowed sisters, with their little babies. One day there came to their tent a visitor who was called Unktomi (spider). He had found some nice red plums during his wanderings in the forest, and he said to himself, "I will keep these plums and fool the two widows with them." After the widows had bidden him be seated, he presented them with the plums.

On seeing them they exclaimed "hi nu, hi nu (an exclamation of surprise), where did you get those fine plums?" Unktomi arose and pointing to a crimson tipped cloud, said: "You see that red cloud? Directly underneath it is a patch of plums. So large is the patch and so red and beautiful are the plums that it is the reflection of them on the cloud that you see."

"Oh, how we wish some one would take care of our babies, while we go over there and pick some," said the sisters. "Why, I am not in any particular hurry, so if you want to go I will take care of my little nephews until you return." (Unktomi always claimed relationship with everyone he met). "Well brother," said the older widow, "take good care of them and we will be back as soon as possible."

The two then took a sack in which to gather the plums, and started off towards the cloud with the crimson lining. Scarcely had they gone from Unktomi's sight when he took the babies out of their swinging hammocks and cut off first one head and then the other. He then took some old blankets and rolled them in the shape of a baby body and laid one in each hammock. Then he took the heads and put them in place in their different hammocks. The bodies he cut up and threw into a large kettle. This he placed over a rousing fire. Then he mixed Indian turnips and arikara squash with the baby meat and soon had a kettle of soup. Just about the time the soup was ready to serve the widows returned. They were tired and hungry and not a plum had they. Unktomi, hearing the approach of the two, hurriedly dished out the baby soup in two wooden dishes and then seated himself near the door so that he could get out easily. Upon the entrance of the widows, Unktomi exclaimed: "Sisters, I had brought some meat with me and I cooked some turnips and squash with it and made a pot of fine soup. The babies have just fallen asleep, so don't waken them until you have finished eating, for I know that you are nearly starved." The two fell to at once and after they had somewhat appeased their appetites, one of them arose and went over to see how her baby was resting. Noting an unnatural color on her baby's face, she raised him up only to have his head roll off from the bundle of blankets. "My son! my son!" she cried out. At once the other hastened to her baby and grabbed it up, only to have the same thing happen. At once they surmised who had done this, and caught up sticks from the fire with which to beat Unktomi to death. He, expecting something like this to happen, lost very little time in getting outside and down into a hole at the roots of a large tree. The two widows not being able to follow Unktomi down into the hole, had to give up trying to get him out, and passed the rest of the day and night crying for their beloved babies. In the meantime Unktomi had gotten out by another opening, and fixing himself up in an entirely different style, and painting his face in a manner that they would not recognize him, he cautiously approached the weeping women and inquired the cause of their tears.

Thus they answered him: "Unktomi came here and fooled us about some plums, and while we were absent killed our babies and made soup out of their bodies. Then he gave us the soup to eat, which we did, and when we found out what he had done we tried to kill him, but he crawled down into that hole and we could not get him out."

"I will get him out," said the mock stranger, and with that he crawled down into the hole and scratched his own face all over to make the widows believe he had been fighting with Unktomi. "I have killed him, and that you may see him

I have enlarged the hole so you can crawl in and see for yourselves, also to take some revenge on his dead body." The two foolish widows, believing him, crawled into the hole, only to be blocked up by Unktomi, who at once gathered great piles of wood and stuffing it into the hole, set it on fire, and thus ended the last of the family who were foolish enough to let Unktomi tempt them with a few red plums.

THE OGRE

Italy

There lived, once upon a time, in the land of Marigliano, a poor woman called Masella, who had six pretty daughters, all as upright as young fir-trees, and an only son called Antonio, who was so simple as to be almost an idiot. Hardly a day passed without his mother saying to him, "What are you doing, you useless creature? If you weren't too stupid to look after yourself, I would order you to leave the house and never to let me see your face again."

Every day the youth committed some fresh piece of folly, till at last Masella, losing all patience, gave him a good beating, which so startled Antonio that he took to his heels and never stopped running till it was dark and the stars were shining in the heavens. He wandered on for some time, not knowing where to go, and at last he came to a cave, at the mouth of which sat an ogre, uglier than anything you can conceive.

He had a huge head and wrinkled brow—eyebrows that met, squinting eyes, a flat broad nose, and a great gash of a mouth from which two huge tusks stuck out. His skin was hairy, his arms enormous, his legs like sword blades, and his feet as flat as ducks'. In short, he was the most hideous and laughable object in the world.

But Antonio, who, with all his faults, was no coward, and was moreover a very civil-spoken lad, took off his hat, and said: "Good-day, sir; I hope you are pretty well. Could you kindly tell me how far it is from here to the place where I wish to go?"

When the ogre heard this extraordinary question he burst out laughing, and as he liked the youth's polite manners he said to him: "Will you enter my service?"

"What wages do you give?" replied Antonio.

"If you serve me faithfully," returned the ogre, "I'll be bound you'll get enough wages to satisfy you."

So the bargain was struck, and Antonio agreed to become the ogre's servant. He was very well treated, in every way, and he had little or no work to do, with the result that in a few days he became as fat as a quail, as round as a barrel, as red as a lobster, and as impudent as a bantam-cock.

But, after two years, the lad got weary of this idle life, and longed desperately to visit his home again. The ogre, who could see into his heart and knew how unhappy he was, said to him one day: "My dear Antonio, I know how much you long to see your mother and sisters again, and because I love you as the apple of my eye, I am willing to allow you to go home for a visit. Therefore, take this donkey, so that you may not have to go on foot; but see that you never say 'Bricklebrit' to him, for if you do you'll be sure to regret it."

Antonio took the beast without as much as saying thank you, and jumping on its back he rode away in great haste; but he hadn't gone two hundred yards when he dismounted and called out: "Bricklebrit."

No sooner had he pronounced the word than the donkey opened its mouth and poured forth rubies, emeralds, diamonds and pearls, as big as walnuts.

Antonio gazed in amazement at the sight of such wealth, and joyfully filling a huge sack with the precious stones, he mounted the donkey again and rode on till he came to an inn. Here he got down, and going straight to the landlord, he said to him: "My good man, I must ask you to stable this donkey for me. Be sure you give the poor beast plenty of oats and hay, but beware of saying the word 'Bricklebrit' to him, for if you do I can promise you will regret it. Take this heavy sack, too, and put it carefully away for me."

The landlord, who was no fool, on receiving this strange warning, and seeing the precious stones sparkling through the canvas of the sack, was most anxious to see what would happen if he used the forbidden word. So he gave Antonio an excellent dinner, with a bottle of fine old wine, and prepared a comfortable bed for him. As soon as he saw the poor simpleton close his eyes and had heard his lusty snores, he hurried to the stables and said to the donkey "Bricklebrit," and the animal as usual poured out any number of precious stones.

When the landlord saw all these treasures he longed to get possession of so valuable an animal, and determined to steal the donkey from his foolish guest. As soon as it was light next morning Antonio awoke, and having rubbed his eyes and stretched himself about a hundred times he called the landlord and said to him: "Come here, my friend, and produce your bill, for short reckonings make long friends."

When Antonio had paid his account he went to the stables and took out his donkey, as he thought, and fastening a sack of gravel, which the landlord had substituted for his precious stones, on the creature's back, he set out for his home.

No sooner had he arrived there than he called out: "Mother, come quickly, and bring table-cloths and sheets with you, and spread them out on the ground, and you will soon see what wonderful treasures I have brought you."

His mother hurried into the house, and opening the linen-chest where she kept her daughters' wedding outfits, she took out table-cloths and sheets made of the finest linen, and spread them flat and smooth on the ground. Antonio placed the donkey on them, and called out "Bricklebrit." But this time he met with no success, for the donkey took no more notice of the magic word than he would have done if a lyre had been twanged in his ear. Two, three, and four times did Antonio pronounce "Bricklebrit," but all in vain, and he might as well have spoken to the wind.

Disgusted and furious with the poor creature, he seized a thick stick and began to beat it so hard that he nearly broke every bone in its body. The miserable donkey was so distracted at such treatment that, far from pouring out precious stones, it only tore and dirtied all the fine linen.

When poor Masella saw her table-cloths and sheets being destroyed, and that instead of becoming rich she had only been made a fool of, she seized another stick and belaboured Antonio so unmercifully with it, that he fled before her, and never stopped till he reached the ogre's cave.

When his master saw the lad returning in such a sorry plight, he understood at once what had happened to him, and making no bones about the matter, he told Antonio what a fool he had been to allow himself to be so imposed upon by the landlord, and to let a worthless animal be palmed off on him instead of his magic donkey.

Antonio listened humbly to the ogre's words, and vowed solemnly that he would never act so foolishly again. And so a year passed, and once more Antonio was overcome by a fit of home-sickness, and felt a great longing to see his own people again.

Now the ogre, although he was so hideous to look upon, had a very kind heart, and when he saw how restless and unhappy Antonio was, he at once gave him leave to go home on a visit. At parting he gave him a beautiful table-cloth, and said: "Give this to your mother; but see that you don't lose it as you lost the donkey, and till you are safely in your own house beware of saying 'Table-cloth, open,' and 'Table-cloth, shut.' If you do, the misfortune be on your own head, for I have given you fair warning."

Antonio set out on his journey, but hardly had he got out of sight of the cave than he laid the table-cloth on the ground and said, "Table-cloth, open." In an instant the table-cloth unfolded itself and disclosed a whole mass of precious stones and other treasures.

When Antonio perceived this he said, "Table-cloth, shut," and continued his journey. He came to the same inn again, and calling the landlord to him, he told him to put the table-cloth carefully away, and whatever he did not to say "Table-cloth, open," or "Table-cloth, shut," to it.

The landlord, who was a regular rogue, answered, "Just leave it to me, I will look after it as if it were my own."

After he had given Antonio plenty to eat and drink, and had provided him with a comfortable bed, he went straight to the table-cloth and said, "Table-cloth, open." It opened at once, and displayed such costly treasures that the landlord made up his mind on the spot to steal it.

When Antonio awoke next morning, the host handed him over a table-cloth exactly like his own, and carrying it carefully over his arm, the foolish youth went straight to his mother's house, and said: "Now we shall be rich beyond the dreams of avarice, and need never go about in rags again, or lack the best of food."

With these words he spread the table-cloth on the ground and said, "Table-cloth, open."

But he might repeat the injunction as often as he pleased, it was only waste of breath, for nothing happened. When Antonio saw this he turned to his mother and said: "That old scoundrel of a landlord has done me once more; but he will live to repent it, for if I ever enter his inn again, I will make him suffer for the loss of my donkey and the other treasures he has robbed me of."

Masella was in such a rage over her fresh disappointment that she could not restrain her impatience, and, turning on Antonio, she abused him soundly, and told him to get out of her sight at once, for she would never acknowledge him as a son of hers again. The poor boy was very depressed by her words, and slunk back to his master like a dog with his tail between his legs. When the ogre saw him, he guessed at once what had happened. He gave Antonio a good scolding, and said, "I don't know what prevents me smashing your head in, you useless ne'er-do-well! You blurt everything out, and your long tongue never ceases wagging for a moment. If you had remained silent in the inn this misfortune would never have overtaken you, so you have only yourself to blame for your present suffering."

Antonio listened to his master's words in silence, looking for all the world like a whipped dog. When he had been three more years in the ogre's service he had another bad fit of home-sickness, and longed very much to see his mother and sisters again.

So he asked for permission to go home on a visit, and it was at once granted to him. Before he set out on his journey the ogre presented him with a beautifully carved stick and said, "Take this stick as a remembrance of me; but beware of saying, 'Rise up, Stick,' and 'Lie down, Stick,' for if you do, I can only say I wouldn't be in your shoes for something."

Antonio took the stick and said, "Don't be in the least alarmed, I'm not such a fool as you think, and know better than most people what two and two make."

"I'm glad to hear it," replied the ogre, "but words are women, deeds are men. You have heard what I said, and forewarned is forearmed."

This time Antonio thanked his master warmly for all his kindness, and started on his homeward journey in great spirits; but he had not gone half a mile when he said "Rise up, Stick."

The words were hardly out of his mouth when the stick rose and began to rain down blows on poor Antonio's back with such lightning-like rapidity that he had hardly strength to call out, "Lie down, Stick"; but as soon as he uttered the words the stick lay down, and ceased beating his back black and blue.

Although he had learnt a lesson at some cost to himself, Antonio was full of joy, for he saw a way now of revenging himself on the wicked landlord. Once more he arrived at the inn, and was received in the most friendly and hospitable manner by his host. Antonio greeted him cordially, and said: "My friend, will you kindly take care of this stick for me? But, whatever you do, don't say 'Rise up, Stick.' If you do, you will be sorry for it, and you needn't expect any sympathy from me."

The landlord, thinking he was coming in for a third piece of good fortune, gave Antonio an excellent supper; and after he had seen him comfortably to bed, he ran to the stick, and calling to his wife to come and see the fun, he lost no time in pronouncing the words "Rise up, Stick."

The moment he spoke the stick jumped up and beat the landlord so unmercifully that he and his wife ran screaming to Antonio, and, waking him up, pleaded for mercy.

When Antonio saw how successful his trick had been, he said: "I refuse to help you, unless you give me all that you have stolen from me, otherwise you will be beaten to death."

The landlord, who felt himself at death's door already, cried out: "Take back your property, only release me from this terrible stick"; and with these words he ordered the donkey, the table-cloth, and other treasures to be restored to their rightful owner.

As soon as Antonio had recovered his belongings he said "Stick, lie down," and it stopped beating the landlord at once.

Then he took his donkey and table-cloth and arrived safely at his home with them. This time the magic words had the desired effect, and the donkey and table-cloth provided the family with treasures untold. Antonio very soon married off his sister, made his mother rich for life, and they all lived happily for ever after.

THE DISOBEDIENT DAUGHTER WHO MARRIED a SKULL

Nigeria

Effiong Edem was a native of Cobham Town. He had a very fine daughter, whose name was Afiong. All the young men in the country wanted to marry her on account of her beauty; but she refused all offers of marriage in spite of repeated entreaties from her parents, as she was very vain, and said she would only marry the best-looking man in the country, who would have to be young and strong, and capable of loving her properly. Most of the men her parents wanted her to marry, although they were rich, were old men and ugly, so the girl continued to disobey her parents, at which they were very much grieved. The Skull who lived in the spirit land heard of the beauty of this Calabar virgin, and thought he would like to possess her; so he went about amongst his friends and borrowed different parts of the body from them, all of the best. From one he got a good head, another lent him a body, a third gave him strong arms, and a fourth lent him a fine pair of legs. At last he was complete, and was a very perfect specimen of manhood.

He then left the spirit land and went to Cobham market, where he saw Afiong, and admired her very much.

About this time Afiong heard that a very fine man had been seen in the market, who was better-looking than any of the natives. She therefore went to the market at once, and directly she saw the Skull in his borrowed beauty, she fell in love with him, and invited him to her house. The Skull was delighted, and went home with her, and on his arrival was introduced by the girl to her parents, and immediately asked their consent to marry their daughter. At first they refused, as they did not wish her to marry a stranger, but at last they agreed.

He lived with Afiong for two days in her parents' house, and then said he wished to take his wife back to his country, which was far off. To this the girl readily agreed, as he was such a fine man, but her parents tried to persuade her not to go. However, being very headstrong, she made up her mind to go, and they started off together. After they had been gone a few days the father consulted his Ju Ju man, who by casting lots very soon discovered that his daughter's husband belonged to the spirit land, and that she would surely be killed. They therefore all mourned her as dead.

After walking for several days, Afiong and the Skull crossed the border between the spirit land and the human country. Directly they set foot in the spirit land, first of all one man came to the Skull and demanded his legs, then another his head, and the next his body, and so on, until in a few minutes the Skull was left by itself in all its natural ugliness. At this the girl was very frightened, and wanted to return home, but the Skull would not allow this, and ordered her to go with him. When they arrived at the Skull's house they found his mother, who was a very old woman quite incapable of doing any work, who could only creep about. Afiong tried her best to help her, and cooked her food, and brought water and firewood for the old woman. The old creature was very grateful for these attentions, and soon became quite fond of Afiong.

One day the old woman told Afiong that she was very sorry for her, but all the people in the spirit land were cannibals, and when they heard there was a human being in their country, they would come down and kill her and eat her. The Skull's mother then hid Afiong, and as she had looked after her so well, she promised she would send her back to her country as soon as possible, providing that she promised for the future to obey her parents. This Afiong readily consented to do. Then the old woman sent for the spider, who was a very clever hairdresser, and made him dress Afiong's hair in the latest fashion. She also presented her with anklets and other things on account of her kindness. She then made a Ju Ju and called the winds to come and convey Afiong to her home. At first a violent tornado came, with thunder, lightning, and rain, but the Skull's mother sent him away as unsuitable. The next wind to come was a gentle breeze, so she told the breeze to carry Afiong to her mother's house, and said good-bye to her. Very soon afterwards the breeze deposited Afiong outside her home, and left her there.

When the parents saw their daughter they were very glad, as they had for some months given her up as lost. The father spread soft animals' skins on the ground from where his daughter was standing all the way to the house, so that her feet should not be soiled. Afiong then walked to the house, and her father called all the young girls who belonged to Afiong's company to come and dance, and the feasting and dancing was kept up for eight days and nights. When the rejoicing was over, the father reported what had happened to the head chief of the town. The chief then passed a law that parents should never allow their daughters to marry strangers who came from a far country. Then the father told his daughter to marry a friend of his, and she willingly consented, and lived with him for many years, and had many children.

A DRAGON'S FAVOUR

ૐ

China

To those who win their favour, the dragons are preservers even when they come forth as destroyers. The story is told of how Wu, the son of a farmer named Yin, won the favour of a dragon and rose to be a great man in China. When he was a boy of thirteen, he was sitting one day at the garden gate, looking across the plain which is watered by a winding river that flows from the mountains. He was a silent, dreamy boy, who had been brought up by his grandmother, his mother having died when he was very young, and it was his habit thus to sit in silence, thinking and observing things. Along the highway came a handsome youth riding a white horse. He was clad in yellow garments and seemed to be of high birth. Four man-servants accompanied him, and one held an umbrella to shield him from the sun's bright rays. The youth drew up his horse at the gate and, addressing Wu, said: "Son of Yin, I am weary. May I enter your father's house and rest a little time."

The boy bowed and said: "Enter."

Yin then came forward and opened the gate. The noble youth dismounted and sat on a seat in the court, while his servants tethered the horse. The farmer chatted with his visitor, and Wu gazed at them in silence. Food was brought, and when the meal was finished, the youth thanked him for his hospitality and walked across the courtyard. Wu noticed that before one of the servants passed through the gate, he turned the umbrella upside down. When the youth had mounted his horse, he turned to the silent, observant boy and said: "I shall come again to-morrow."

Wu bowed and answered: "Come!"

The strangers rode away, and Wu sat watching them until they had vanished from sight.

When evening came on, the farmer spoke to his son regarding the visitors, and said: "The noble youth knew my name and yet I have never set eyes on him before."

Wu was silent for a time. Then he said: "I cannot say who the youth is or who his attendants are."

"You watched them very closely, my son. Did you note anything peculiar about them?"

Said Wu: "There were no seams in their clothing; the white horse had spots of five colours and scaly armour instead of hair. The hoofs of the horse and the feet of the strangers did not touch the ground."[1]

Yin rose up with agitation and exclaimed: "Then they are not human beings, but spirits."

Said Wu: "I watched them as they went westward. Rain-clouds were gathering on the horizon, and when they were a great distance off they all rose in the air and vanished in the clouds."[2]

Yin was greatly alarmed to hear this, and said: "I must ask your grandmother what she thinks of this strange happening."

The old woman was fast asleep, and as she had grown very deaf it was difficult to awaken her. When at length she was thoroughly roused, and sat up with head and hands trembling with palsy,[3] Yin repeated to her in a loud voice all that Wu had told him.

Said the woman: "The horse, spotted with five colours, and with scaly armour instead of hair, is a dragon-horse. When spirits appear before human beings they wear magic garments. That is why the clothing of your visitors had no seams. Spirits tread on air. As these spirits went westward, they rose higher and higher

---

1. A similar belief regarding supernatural beings prevailed in India. Sec story of Nala in *Indian Myth and Legend.*
2. The appearance of four servants (the gods of the four quarters) with the dragon-god, indicates that the coming storm is to be one of exceptional violence.
3. The deep slumberer in a folk-tale is usually engaged "working a spell." As will be gathered from the story, the boy received his knowledge and power from his grandmother. She resembles the Norse Vala and the Witch of Endor.

in the air, going towards the rain-clouds. The youth was the Yellow Dragon. He is to raise a storm, and as he had four followers the storm will be a great one. May no evil befall us."

Then Yin told the old woman that one of the strangers had turned the umbrella upside down before passing through the garden gate. "That is a good omen," she said. Then she lay down and closed her eyes. "I have need of sleep," she murmured; "I am very old."[4]

Heavy masses of clouds were by this time gathering in the sky, and Yin decided to sit up all night. Wu asked to be permitted to do the same, and his father consented. Then the boy lit a yellow lantern, put on a yellow robe that his grandmother had made for him, burned incense, and sat down reading charms from an old yellow book.[5]

The storm burst forth in fury just when dawn was breaking dimly. Wu then closed his yellow book and went to a window. The thunder bellowed, the lightning flamed, and the rain fell in torrents, and swollen streams poured down from the mountains. Soon the river rose in flood and swept across the fields. Cattle gathered in groups on shrinking mounds that had become islands surrounded by raging water.

Yin feared greatly that the house would be swept away, and wished he had fled to the mountains.

At night the cottage was entirely surrounded by the flood. Trees were cast down and swept away. "We cannot escape now," groaned Yin.

Wu sat in silence, displaying no signs of emotion. "What do you think of it all?" his father asked.

Wu reminded him that one of the strangers had turned the umbrella upside down, and added: "Before the dragon youth went away he spoke and said: 'I shall come again to-morrow'."

"He has come indeed," Yin groaned, and covered his face with his hands.

---

4. The Norse Vala makes similar complaint when awakened by Odin. It looks as if this Chinese story is based on one about consulting a spirit of a "wise woman" who sleeps in her tomb.
5. An interesting glimpse of the connection between colour symbolism and magic. Everything is yellow because a yellow dragon is being invoked.

Said Wu: "I have just seen the dragon. As I looked towards the sky he spread out his great hood above our home. He is protecting us now."

"Alas! my son, you are dreaming."

"Listen, father, no rain falls on the roof."

Yin listened intently. Then he said: "You speak truly, my son. This is indeed a great marvel."

"It was well," said Wu, "that you welcomed the dragon yesterday."

"He spoke to you first, my son; and you answered, 'Enter.' Ah, you have much wisdom. You will become a great man."

The storm began to subside, and Wu prevailed upon his father to lie down and sleep.[6]

Much damage had been done by storm and flood, and large numbers of human beings and domesticated animals had perished. In the village, which was situated at the mouth of the valley, only a few houses were left standing.

The rain ceased to fall at midday. Then the sun came out and shone brightly, while the waters began to retreat.

Wu went outside and sat at the garden gate, as was his custom. In time he saw the yellow youth returning from the west, accompanied by his four attendants. When he came nigh, Wu bowed and the youth drew up his horse and spoke, saying: "I said I should return to-day."

Wu bowed.

"But this time I shall not enter the courtyard," the youth added.

"As you will," Wu said reverently.

The dragon youth then handed the boy a single scale which he had taken from the horse's neck, and said: "Keep this and I shall remember you."

Then he rode away and vanished from sight.

The boy re-entered the house. He awoke his father and said: "The storm is over and the dragon has returned to his pool."[7]

---

6.   This sleep appears to be as necessary as that of the grandmother.

7.   The latest spell had been worked, and it was not necessary that the father should sleep any longer.

Yin embraced his son, and together they went to inform the old woman. She awoke, sat up, and listened to all that was said to her. When she learned that the dragon youth had again appeared and had spoken to Wu, she asked: "Did he give you ought before he departed?"

Wu opened a small wooden box and showed her the scale that had been taken from the neck of the dragon horse.

The woman was well pleased, and said: "When the Emperor sends for you, all will be well."

Yin was astonished to hear these words, and exclaimed: "Why should the Emperor send for my boy?"

"You shall see," the old woman made answer as she lay down again.

Before long the Emperor heard of the great marvel that had been worked in the flooded valley. Men who had taken refuge on the mountains had observed that no rain fell on Yin's house during the storm. So His Majesty sent couriers to the valley, and these bade Yin to accompany them to the palace, taking Wu with him.

On being brought before the Emperor, Yin related everything that had taken place. Then His Majesty asked to see the scale of the dragon horse.

It was growing dusk when Wu opened the box, and the scale shone so brightly that it illumined the throne-room so that it became as bright as at high noon.

Said the Emperor: "Wu shall remain here and become one of my magicians. The yellow dragon has imparted to him much power and wisdom."

Thus it came about that Wu attained high rank in the kingdom. He found that great miracles could be worked with the scale of the dragon horse. It cured disease, and it caused the Emperor's army to win victories. Withal, Wu was able to foretell events, and he became a renowned prophet and magician.

The farmer's son grew to be very rich and powerful. A great house was erected for him close to the royal palace, and he took his grandmother and father to it, and there they lived happily until the end of their days.

Thus did Wu, son of Yin, become a great man, because of the favour shown to him by the thunder-dragon, who had wrought great destruction in the river valley and taken toll of many lives.

A NOTE ON THE SOURCES

The stories in this book were collected, translated, and published in the late nineteenth and early twentieth centuries. They have been excerpted from the following publications, all of which are in the public domain.

In most cases, the authors either completed the transcription and translation themselves or worked with unnamed interpreters. The storytellers also generally remain unnamed. There are a few exceptions.

The stories presented in *Japanese Fairy Tales* were translated by Yei Theodora Ozaki from original accounts by Sadanami Sanjin and Shinsui Tamenaga, as well as a story from the classic work *Taketori Monogatari*.

In *The Grey Fairy Book* and *The Violet Fairy Book*, Andrew Lang curated the selections, and the translations were done by Leonora Lang, Miss Eleanor Sellar, and Mr. W. A. Craigie, as well as Mrs. Dent, Miss Blackley, and Miss Hang (for whom no first names are given). "The Ogre and The Goblin Pony" were translated from texts by Hermann Kletke, and "The Young Man Who Would Have His Eyes Opened" was translated from a text by Friedrich Kreuzwald.

For *Cossack Fairy Tales*, R. Nisbet Bain translated stories from the publications of Panteleimon Kulish, Ivan Rudchenko, and Mykhaylo Dragomanov.

One story in this book is a contemporary translation of an old text. "The Demon's Daughter" was translated from the French by Mirabelle Korn in 2019 for this collection.

SOURCES

"The Bird of Sorrow"
Kúnos, Ignácz. *Forty-Four Turkish Fairy Tales.* Reprint of the George G Harrap & Co. 1913 London edition, Internet Archive, 2007. https://archive.org/details/fortyfourturkish001862/page/n5.

"The Blood-Drawing Ghost"
Curtin, Jeremiah. *Tales of the Fairies and of the Ghost World.* Reprint of the Little, Brown & Company 1895 Boston edition, Internet Archive, 2009. https://archive.org/details/talesfairiesand00curtgoog/page/n9.

"The Buso-Monkey"
Benedict, Laura Watson. *Bagobo Myths.* Reprint of the January 1913 Journal of American Folk-lore, Internet Archive, 2013. https://archive.org/details/jstor-534786/page/n1.

"The Demon's Daughter" [originally published as "La fille du démon"]
Oestrup, J. *Contes de Damas.* Reprint of the E. J. Brill 1897 Leyde edition, Internet Archive, 2008. https://archive.org/details/contesdedamasrec00stuoft.

"The Disobedient Daughter Who Married a Skull"
Dayrell, Elphinstone. *Folk Stories from Southern Nigeria, West Africa.* Reprint of the Longmans, Green and Co. 1910 London edition, Internet Archive, 2008. https://archive.org/details/folkstoriesfroms00dayrrich/page/n8.

"A Dragon's Favour" [originally published without a title]
Mackenzie, Donald A. *Myths of China and Japan.* Reprint of the Gresham Publishing Company 1923 London edition, Internet Archive, 2008. https://archive.org/details/mythsofchinajapa00mack/page/94.

"The Draiglin' Hogney"
Grierson, Elizabeth W., *The Scottish Fairy Book.* Reprint of the J. B. Lippincott Company 1910 Philadelphia edition, Internet Archive, 2007. https://archive.org/details/scottishfairyboo00grie/page/n8.

"The Goblin Pony"
The Grey Fairy Book. Edited by Andrew Lang. Reprint of the Longmans, Green and Co. 1905 New York edition, Internet Archive, 2007. https://archive.org/details/greyfairybook00lang/page/n10.

"Kiviung"
Boas, Franz. *The Central Eskimo.* Reprint of the Bureau of Ethnology sixth annual report, pl. II, Smithsonian Institution, Washington, 1888. Project Gutenberg, 2013. http://www.gutenberg.org/files/42084/42084-h/42084-h.htm#tales_narwhal.

"The Iron Wolf"
Bain, R. Nisbet. *Cossack Fairy Tales.* Reprint of the George G. Harrap & Co. 1916 Kingsway W. C. edition, Internet Archive, 2007. https://archive.org/details/cossack-fairytale00bain/page/n9.

"The Man-Whale"
Arnason, Jón, *Icelandic Legends.* Translated by George E. J. Powell and Eiríkur Magnússon. Reprint of the Richard Bentley 1864 London edition. Internet Archive, 2009. https://archive.org/details/icelandiclegend02powegoog.

"The Mermaid's Lake"
Dance, Rev. Charles Daniel. *Chapters from a Guianese Log-Book.* Reprint of the Royal Gazette Establishment 1881 Georgetown, Demerara edition, Google Books, 2019. https://books.google.com/books?id=r7UNAAAAQAAJ&printsec=frontcover&source=gbs_ge_summary_r&cad=0#v=onepage&q&f=false.

"My Lord Bag of Rice"
Ozaki, Yei Theodora. *Japanese Fairy Tales.* Reprint of the Grosset & Dunlap 1908 New York edition, Internet Archive, 2007. https://archive.org/details/japanesefairytal00ozak.

"Nya-Nya Bulembu; or, the Moss-Green Princess"
Bourhill, Mrs. E. J. and Mrs. J. B. Drake. *Fairy Tales from South Africa.* Reprint of the Macmillan and Co. 1908 London edition, Internet Archive, 2006. https://archive.org/details/fairytalesfromso00bourrich/page/n9.

"The Ogre"
The Grey Fairy Book. Edited by Andrew Lang. Reprint of the Longmans, Green and Co. 1905 New York edition, Internet Archive, 2007. https://archive.org/details/greyfairybook00lang/page/n10 .

"The Origin of the Narran Lake"
Langloh Parker, K. *Australian Legendary Tales*. Reprint of the David Nutt 1896 London edition, Internet Archive, 2009. https://archive.org/details/cu31924029909060/page/n6.

"The Princess and the Ghouls"
[originally published as "The Princess and the Ogres"]
Swynnerton, Charles, *Indian Nights' Entertainment; or, Folk-Tales from the Upper Indus*. Reprint of the Elliot Stock 1892 London edition, Internet Archive, 2009. https://archive.org/details/cu31924023651072.

"The Sobbing Pine"
Lummis, Charles F. *Pueblo Indian Folk-Stories*. Reprint of the D. Appleton-Century Company 1936 New York & London edition, Internet Archive, 2007. https://archive.org/details/puebloindianfolk00lumm/page/n5.

"The Three Chests: The Story of the Wicked Old Man of the Sea"
Fillmore, Parker, *Mighty Mikko: A Book of Finnish Fairy Tales and Folk Tales*. Reprint of the Harcourt, Brace and Company 1922 New York edition, Internet Archive, 2007. https://archive.org/details/mightymikkobooko00fill.

"The Unktomi (Spider), Two Widows, and the Red Plums"
McLaughlin, Marie L. *Myths and Legends of the Sioux*. Reprint of the Bismarck Tribune Company 1916 Bismark N. D. edition, Internet Archive, 2019. https://archive.org/details/b31352741/page/n6.

"The Young Man Who Would Have His Eyes Opened"
The Violet Fairy Book. Edited by Andrew Lang. Reprint of the Longmans, Green and Co. 1906 New York edition, Internet Archive, 2007. https://archive.org/details/violetfairybook00lang/page/n10.